"You never g

Christian accused. "I know why I'm being wined and dined by the best-looking woman in Atlanta." He looked down at her, his expression hard. "But it won't work. I have no interest in your project."

A flush colored Laurel's cheeks. "I'll admit I thought if we got to know each other better—"

"How much better?" He gripped her arms and pulled her up against him. "How far did you plan to go in your attempt to convince me? A few kisses in the line of duty? Perhaps a nightcap in your room to seal the bargain?"

"No!" Laurel cried, tears stinging her eyes.

"Why did you ask me out, Laurel?"

"I wanted . . ."

He tilted her chin up so they were almost eye to eye. "Was this why?" he asked, sending a shock wave through her at the touch of his lips against hers.

Dear Reader,

Welcome to Silhouette **Special Edition** ... welcome to romance. Each month, Silhouette **Special Edition** publishes six novels with you in mind—stories of love and life, tales that you can identify with—as well as dream about.

And this wonderful month of May has many terrific stories for you. Myrna Temte presents her contribution to THAT SPECIAL WOMAN!—our new promotion that salutes women, and the wonderful men who win them. *The Forever Night* features characters you met in her COWBOY COUNTRY series—as well as a romance for sheriff Andy Johnson, whom many of you have written in about. Ginny Bradford gets her man in this gentle tale of love.

This month also brings *He's the Rich Boy* by Lisa Jackson. This is the concluding tale to her MAVERICKS series that features men that just won't be tamed! Don't miss this tale of love at misty Whitefire Lake!

Rounding out this special month are books from other favorite authors: Barbara Faith, Pat Warren, Kayla Daniels and Patricia McLinn—who is back with *Grady's Wedding* (you remember Grady—he was an usher in *Wedding Party*, #718. Now he has his own tale of love!).

I hope that you enjoy this book, and all the stories to come. Have a wonderful month!

Sincerely,

Tara Gavin
Senior Editor
Silhouette Books

BARBARA FAITH

THIS ABOVE ALL

Silhouette®

SPECIAL EDITION®

Published by Silhouette Books New York

America's Publisher of Contemporary Romance

To Paula Detmer Riggs, with a great deal of love.

SILHOUETTE BOOKS
300 East 42nd St., New York, N.Y. 10017

THIS ABOVE ALL

Copyright © 1993 by Barbara Faith

ISBN: 0-373-09812-X

First Silhouette Books printing May 1993

Printed in the U.S.A.

BARBARA FAITH

is a true romantic who believes that love is a rare and precious gift. She has an endless fascination with the attraction a man and a woman from different cultures and backgrounds have for each other. She considers herself a good example of such an attraction, because she has been happily married for twenty years to an ex-matador she met when she lived in Mexico.

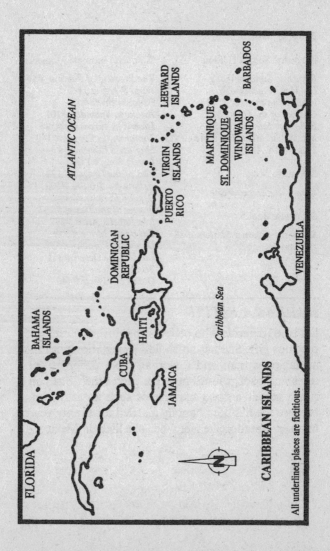

CARIBBEAN ISLANDS

All underlined places are fictitious.

Chapter One

He was probably the most attractive man she had ever seen. Tall, but not too tall, slender, but not thin, there was something about him, something in his eyes and the proud stance of his body, that suggested an animal magnetism, a powerful quality that excited and intrigued her.

Eli Dorset, President and CEO of the Grand Dorset Hotels, introduced them.

"Laurel, this is Christian Dumond," Eli said. "Minister of Commerce and Trade in St. Dominique. Monsieur Dumond, Laurel Merritt is our Vice President of Public Relations."

He took her hand. His skin was smooth and tanned. "Miss Merritt," he said, with the barest suggestion of a French accent.

They spoke only a few words before Enrique Cervantes, who owned and operated a hotel in Bogotá, interrupted to say, "Come along, Christian, I want you to meet some friends from Quito."

"Please excuse me, Miss Merritt." He took her hand again. For a moment his eyes met hers, but it was enough.

Laurel watched him from across the room. Once or twice he turned to look at her and when he did he inclined his head, acknowledging that he had seen her before he returned to the group surrounding him.

"Dumond's the main reason for having the conference," Eli said, helping himself to the hors d'oeuvres. "He has a say in where, and if, we build our complex and he's playing hardball. Laurel, I want you to zero in on him. St. Dominique is ripe for a multimillion-dollar resort and we're going to build one before anybody else does."

"I know he's been hesitating," Laurel said, "but I don't know why."

"Neither do we. Sugarcane and tourism are St. Dominique's two main sources of income. A resort like the kind we'd build would bring millions of dollars to the island." Eli bit into a cheese ball. "Why don't you get him away from here tomorrow? Take him to lunch. Show him the countryside. Try to convince him that a Grand Dorset resort is just what St. Dominique needs." He raised his glass to Laurel's. "There's a bonus in it for you," he added.

She looked toward Dumond. There were fewer women than men at tonight's reception, but the ones who were there had managed to maneuver their way to stand near him. From where Laurel watched, it seemed that enough eyelashes were being fluttered to start a minor hurricane.

"I'll do my best," she told Eli Dorset and, with a smile, started across the room. When she drew closer to Dumond she took two champagne glasses off the proffered tray of a passing waiter.

"I'm terribly sorry," she told the women surrounding him like hens around a prize rooster, "but I'm afraid I have to steal Mr. Dumond away." She handed him one of the champagne glasses, then linked her arm through his and before either he or the ladies could voice an objection, steered him toward the French doors that opened onto the balcony.

"It's a warm night, Monsieur Dumond," she said. "I thought it was time you had a breath of our good Georgia air."

"Merci," he said, with the barest suggestion of a smile.

"Have you ever been to Atlanta before?"

Dumond shook his head. "This is my first visit, Miss Merritt."

"Laurel," she said.

"Laurel." Softly spoken in a French accent.

She took a deep breath. "I've never been to St. Dominique. Only to Jamaica and Barbados. Tell me about your island."

"My island?" He looked out over the lights of Atlanta. "The travel brochures describe it as a tropical paradise, a foreign land of grace and enchantment and perpetual summer. The sun warms you during the day and the trade winds cool you at night."

He turned to look at Laurel. "It's a mystical island," he said.

"You were born there?"

Dumond nodded. "I have lived in other places, but St. Dominique will always be my home."

"Other places?" she asked, curious.

"I went to school at the Sorbonne in Paris." He took a sip of his champagne. "And later here in your country."

"Where?"

"North Carolina."

"Did you like it there?"

"It was all right."

"Tell me more about St. Dominique," she said. "Not just the tourist things."

"Logistics?" Dumond shrugged, then recited, "Located in the Lesser Antilles, it is more than five hundred square miles in area, served by roads that wind up into the mountains and along the coast. We have a population of over a quarter of a million. Roughly eighty-five per cent are descendants of African slaves and the Carib Indians. The French came in the late 1600s to conquer the Caribs and import slaves from Africa to work in the sugarcane fields."

She watched his face as he talked. His features were smooth and unlined. His close-cropped black hair was curly, his eyes dove gray. His teeth were a startling white. He was clean-shaven.

"It's a beautiful country," he said. "I think it's the most beautiful of all the Caribbean islands."

"Then it's the perfect place for the kind of resort we want to build." Laurel smiled her million-dollar smile. "Our chief architect has already started on the plans. I've seen them and I think you'll be pleased."

Christian Dumond shook his head. "I don't think so."

"But you haven't seen them," Laurel protested.

"I'm not saying no to the plans, Miss Merritt. I'm saying no to a resort of the kind your company wants to build."

"But why?"

"We have enough tourist hotels on the island. We don't need any more."

"Grand Dorset doesn't build tourist hotels, Mr. Dumond. We build complete resorts. The plans I've seen include tennis courts, swimming pools with swim-up bars, terraced gardens, bungalows, as well as what will be a truly magnificent hotel." She took a sip of her champagne. "From what Mr. Ginsburg—he's the architect—has told me, the land that has been chosen is one of the most beautiful on St. Dominique. It overlooks the sea and—"

"No!" Dumond's expression hardened. "Not that piece of land."

Laurel hesitated. She looked down on the lights of the city and wondered how in the world she was going to convince Dumond to do something he obviously didn't want to do. Eli had made up his mind that he was going to build on St. Dominique, and usually when Eli's mind was made up it was a fait accompli. He'd spent a week on St. Dominique a year ago and he'd been talking about it ever since. Two months ago he'd sent Victor Reiger, head of international sales, and Hal Ginsburg to the island. When they returned they'd raved about the site they'd found overlooking the sea.

"It's a magnificent place," Hal had told them at the meeting Eli had held the day after they'd returned. "Twenty-five acres of tropical paradise. We'd build the hotel on the cliff overlooking the sea, with terraces down toward the water. I envision a waterfall running from pool to pool, lit at night with different colored lights sparkling across the water. And a discotheque with enough electric guitars to be heard all the way to Jamaica."

"It will be the finest resort of its kind in the Caribbean," Reiger had added. "Tourists will come in droves and Grand Dorset will make millions of dollars over the next five or ten years. But..." he'd looked at Eli Dorset "...first we have to convince this guy Dumond. There are other monied interests who are all for the idea, but without Dumond's okay there won't be a resort."

"We'll convince him," Eli Dorset had said.

And though ostensibly the party tonight had been arranged for all of the tourist reps from the Caribbean and South America, the main purpose had been to get Christian Dumond here and to persuade him to let Dorset build their resort on St. Dominique.

Laurel looked at the set face, the mouth drawn into a tight line, and wondered how in the world she could convince this man of anything. But she had to try; it was her job to try. It wouldn't be easy but she was, as her mother had often told her, a Southern woman.

"We have an advantage over other women, honey," Darcie Ann always said, half joking, half serious. "We're honeysuckle and roses, baby. We can charm the socks off a man at fifty paces."

Laurel took a deep breath. "It's too nice a night to talk business," she said in what she hoped was her best honeysuckle-and-roses voice. She smiled up at him. "I'm in charge of public relations, Mr. Dumond. It's my job to make sure you're having a good time. If you don't want to talk business, then we'll talk about something else."

A waiter paused at the open French doors and she motioned to him. With a smile she took the empty champagne glass out of Christian's hand and handed him a fresh one. "Let's drink to a steamy night in Georgia," she said and, never taking her eyes off him, touched her glass to his.

He had heard about Southern women and when he'd gone to Duke he'd met his share of them. But this woman was different. She spoke in the soft drawl he had heard before in the South, but in her voice there was a hint of teasing sensuality that made him want to know her better.

She was a very pretty young woman, with flawless skin that made him think of the pink camellias that grew on St. Dominique. Her eyes were a pale turquoise, her lips were full and ripe. She was of medium height, with nicely rounded breasts, a small waist and narrow hips. She wore a long-sleeved white organza blouse and a full-length black silk skirt. Elegant, understated and ladylike, until you realized that the sleeves of the blouse were so sheer you could see the outline of her delicate arms, and that the cascade of ruffles almost, but not quite, disguised the enticing décolletage. Whenever she turned he would catch just a glimpse of her breasts, and when she moved her head the ruffles caressed the pale softness of her throat.

She was a delectable woman from the top of her smooth blond hair all the way down to the tips of her black satin shoes. And if he had half a brain he'd have absolutely nothing else to do with her.

"Mr. Dumond?"

He looked at her, startled. "I'm sorry," he said. "Did you say something?"

"I said I'd like to take you to lunch tomorrow. There's a French restaurant I think you'd enjoy. Afterward we could drive out into the country." Laurel smiled her most winning smile. "Conferences like this can be a bore after a day or two. And believe me, there's nothing prettier than springtime in Georgia." Her voice held a hint of laughter. "I'll even promise not to talk business."

"Well, I..." Christian hesitated.

"Twelve-thirty?" she said. "In the lobby?"

He knew he should say that he was sorry, that he had already made other plans. But just then the clouds glided away and the moon came out to touch her face in a way that stopped the breath in his throat.

He took a sip of his champagne. "Twelve-thirty."

Her hair was loose about her face. She had on a blue cotton, full-skirted gypsy dress and high-heeled white sandals. Her bare legs were long and sleek and beautiful.

"Hi," Laurel said, and her voice sounded like springtime. "Isn't it a beautiful day? We'll have lunch first and then I'm going to show you some of our nice Georgia countryside."

They went outside the hotel. Someone had already brought her car around and Christian was not surprised to see that it was a bright red convertible. Of course, he thought, as he got in beside her.

The restaurant was charming; the food delicious. She ordered a cool white wine and when she touched her glass to his, said, "To St. Dominique."

"You must come for a visit."

"I intend to."

"To try to talk me into giving you that piece of land you're after?"

"I'm not after the land," she said. "Grand Dorset is."

"Isn't that the same thing?"

"I'm a loyal employee. I do what I'm told."

He cocked an eyebrow. "Always?" he asked.

She grinned. "Almost always." Then her expression changed. "Why don't you want the resort on St. Dominique?"

"I thought we weren't going to talk business."

"I really want to know."

"I don't approve of the place your people want to put the resort."

"But why?"

He drummed long slender fingers against the white tablecloth. "A long time ago that particular place belonged to the Carib Indians. In my opinion it still does."

"Do any of them live there?"

"No."

"But if they don't live there..." Laurel shook her head. "I don't understand," she said.

"It was their ancestral land," Christian told her. "To them and to the blacks who came later it's sacred."

"If they don't live there, then, I can't understand why you don't want to sell it." She leaned across the table and he caught the scent of her perfume, light floral with just a hint of musk.

"Don't you realize what a resort like the kind Dorset wants to build would do for your island?" she asked. "It would bring in millions of dollars every year in tourists' money, Mr. Dumond. It would—"

"My name is Christian," he said.

She fascinated him. He knew that she had invited him to lunch today only because of the land, and that very likely she would persist, using all of her undeniable charms in an effort to get what she wanted. He'd known that last night, yet he had agreed to come today. And now that he was here he could not take his eyes off her.

When the check came he tried to pay it. But she said, "This is on Dorset," and he watched, amused, when she handed her plastic card to the waiter.

American women, he thought.

They drove for over an hour. The top was down. The sky was a clear, clean blue and the air was scented with spring flowers. Laurel was glad that Eli had asked her to get Christian away from the hotel today. He was a handsome and interesting man, someone she wanted to know better, and not just because of the resort Dorset wanted to build on his island.

"I'm glad you agreed to come out with me today," she said.

"So am I."

Last night she had looked sleek and sophisticated, but she was different today with the sunlight on her face and her blond hair blowing in the wind. He could not see the expression in her eyes because of the dark sunglasses she wore, but he knew by the way her mouth turned up at the corners that she was smiling and enjoying the day, as he was.

They had left the main highway almost an hour ago and the road they were now traveling on passed Georgia red farmland. Cows grazed in newly green pastures, and farmers rode their tractors, with their straw hats pushed back on their foreheads to let the sun warm their faces.

"I think I'll show you where I was born and raised," Laurel said. She hadn't intended to, but suddenly it seemed like a good idea. They could relax on the veranda, maybe have a drink or two, and she wouldn't talk business until they started back to Atlanta.

"If we're lucky we might just be in time for a mint julep," she said. "Euphemia makes the best in the county."

"Euphemia?"

"Mama's maid. She's been with the family since I was born. We couldn't get along without her."

"You don't still live all the way out here, do you?"

Laurel shook her head. "No, I have an apartment in town. But I get out whenever I can. I like the country atmosphere. And I reckon I like being waited on."

"Spoiled," Christian Dumond said with a smile.

"You bet."

She smiled back at him and suddenly, inexplicably, he wanted to touch her. And because he did, he looked away and said, "Tell me about your family."

"My dad died when I was eleven," she said. "After that everybody tried to talk Mama into selling the house and moving to either Atlanta or Macon. But she decided to stay out here in the country. The house belonged to her father and his father before him. It's a lovely old place. That's why I thought you might enjoy seeing it."

"Does your mother live alone?"

"No, my sister Virgie, Virginia, lives with her. She's three years younger than I am."

"Is she as pretty as you are?" he asked, and wished he hadn't.

Laurel laughed, and the sound of it made him smile again.

"Virgie's the pretty one in the family," she said. "She looks like Mama. People say that I look more like my father, but I don't know. I don't guess I remember him all that well."

She turned off the road they were traveling, onto a smaller graveled road lined with great white oaks. He saw the word Private printed on a large post, and just ahead an iron fence. When they reached the gate Laurel took a small cassettelike box out of the glove compartment, punched it, and the gate opened automatically.

"There's the house," she said. "Through the trees." And he saw it, white pillared and stately, set back on a rolling green lawn surrounded by willow trees.

"I can see why your mother didn't want to sell it," he said.

"Yes, so can I." Laurel took off her dark glasses and stopped for a moment, looking toward the home where she had grown up. "Daddy took me to see *Gone With the Wind* when I was seven. For months afterward I insisted on calling our home Tara. And every time I got mad at somebody I'd mutter, 'Damn Yankee!'"

Christian laughed, liking her more every minute.

"My great-grandfather named this place White Oaks," she said, and started the car, anxious now to see her mother and sister, anxious in a way she could not explain for them to meet Christian Dumond.

They were on the veranda when she drove the car into the circular driveway and stopped.

"Darlin'!" Darcie Ann jumped up and like a bright pink butterfly fluttered down the wide front steps. "Whyever didn't you call? You should have let us know you were coming." She stopped to stare at Christian, fluffed her hair away from the back of her neck, and said, "I didn't know you were bringing a guest."

"This is Christian Dumond, Mother. Christian, this is my mother, Darcie Ann Merritt."

He got out of the car and came around. "Mrs. Merritt," he said. *"Enchanté,"* and when she offered her hand he kissed it.

"You're French!" she exclaimed, looking absolutely delighted.

"Christian is from St. Dominique in the Caribbean," Laurel said.

"I do declare." Virgie stood on the top step, one shoulder leaning against a round column, pale as a Cherokee rose in tight white silk pants and an off-the-shoulder white blouse. She gave Christian a sloe-eyed look. "I'm Virgie," she said. "Laurel's younger sister. Welcome to the marbled halls."

"Merci." He opened Laurel's door and held his hand out to her. "This is a lovely home, Mrs. Mer-

ritt," he said to her mother. "I'm glad Laurel wanted to show it to me."

"Well, so am I." Darcie Ann linked her arm through his. "We were just about to have tea but I'd be happy to fetch something stronger if you'd prefer it."

"No, thank you. Tea is fine."

"I thought the English drank tea and the French drank wine." Virgie uncurled herself from the white column and eased into one of the white wicker chairs. "You have a marvelous tan," she said.

"Thank you." His lips curved in the slightest suggestion of a smile.

"Laurel likes to get out in the sun but I never do. My skin is too delicate. I have to be very careful." She moved her chair closer to his. "Tell me all about where you come from," she said.

Laurel watched with a glint of interest and a soupçon of anger. Always before she had been amused by Virgie's flirting. Now she found she wasn't amused. That surprised her. There was a part of her that thought, I should have known better than to have brought him home, and another part of her that was curious to know how Christian would react to Virgie.

He drank his tea. He smiled at Virgie. He acted politely, as though he were an elderly uncle, tolerantly amused by a rather precocious niece.

Virgie didn't realize it, at least not at first. But after a while her finely plucked eyebrows came together and the barest hint of a frown pursed her lips. She slipped the off-the-shoulder blouse a little lower and moved closer.

"You sure you wouldn't like a drink, darlin'?" she asked Christian.

"No, thank you."

"Well, I would." She smiled at him, then called out, "Euphemia! Where in the blazes are you, woman?"

"Virgie," Darcie Ann chided, indicating the little silver bell on the table. "You could have rung for her." She smiled at Christian. "Euphemia's our colored maid," she said. "She's been with us for years."

"We shouldn't have to ring," Virgie said with a frown. "She should have come running the minute we all sat down. She's getting so old she's hardly any use at all. Seems to me..."

Virgie stopped and glared at the black woman coming toward her across the wide porch. She was tall and slim, wearing a light green cotton dress with white collar and cuffs. Her gray hair was neatly done up in a bun at the back of her head. And her eyes were snapping with anger.

"You yelled?" she said to Virgie.

"I *called,*" Virgie snapped. "We have a guest and—"

"Miss Laurel!" The woman's face softened into a smile. "I was out back and I didn't hear you drive up. You should have let me know you were here."

"Hi, Euphemia." Laurel got up and went to put her arms around the other woman. "How're you doing?"

"I'm doing just fine, 'specially now that you're here."

"I'd like you to meet a friend of mine," Laurel said. "This is Mr. Dumond, Euphemia. He's from the island of St. Dominique."

Euphemia looked at him. Her eyebrows drew together and she frowned. "How do you do."

"How do you do," Christian answered.

"Bring me a bourbon," Virgie said. "On the rocks. No water."

"It's a little early in the day, isn't it?" Darcie Ann asked.

"No, Mama, it isn't." Virgie shot a look at Laurel. "How about you?"

"I'll stick to tea," Laurel said.

"On your best behavior I see." Virgie laughed, and to Euphemia she said, "Well, don't just stand there. Get my drink."

"You've no right speaking to Euphemia like that," Laurel said in a low voice when the other woman disappeared into the house.

"And you've no right telling me what to do."

"Girls!" Darcie Ann fluttered her hands, and with a chuckle turned to Christian and said, "I swear, this is the way they've been since they were toddlers. But it doesn't mean a thing. It's just sister talk."

Euphemia returned with Virgie's drink. She plunked it down, looked at Christian, and marched off, her back ramrod straight. Later she came out to set the table with a bright red cloth, fine china plates, and crystal wineglasses.

The afternoon lengthened into a lingering twilight. And finally Euphemia served their dinner: baked country ham, potato salad, corn-and-red-pepper relish, hot biscuits and blueberry cobbler.

"You're a wonder, Euphemia." Laurel put her arm around the woman's waist. "It's your good cooking that keeps me coming back so often."

"And all the time I thought it was because of me," Virgie said.

When it was time to leave Darcie Ann drew Laurel inside. "Tell me all about him," she said.

"There's nothing to tell, Mama. I met Christian last night at the reception for travel agents and reps. Dorset wants to build a resort on St. Dominique and it's my job to convince Christian that it's a good idea."

"He certainly is good-looking." Darcie Ann looked at herself in the mirror and fluffed out her hair. "Is he rich?"

"I really don't know."

"How long is he going to be here?"

"I'm not sure. The conference ends the day after tomorrow but I have a hunch Eli's going to try to talk Christian into staying a few days longer. He's determined to build on St. Dominique and it's up to Christian whether he does or not."

"And up to you?"

Laurel smiled at her mother. "Perhaps."

When they went back onto the porch Virgie had once again pulled her chair close to Christian's. She was leaning over him, her long blond hair brushing his hand, and as they approached, Laurel heard her say, "I'll be in Atlanta tomorrow night."

"It's time we started back," Laurel said. "It'll be dark soon and we have an almost two-hour drive."

"Yes, of course." Christian got up, and turning to Darcie Ann said, "I've enjoyed the afternoon and the evening, Mrs. Merritt. The dinner was delicious."

"Why, thank you, Christian. Y'all come back anytime, you hear? It's been a real pleasure meeting a man like you. I've always said that the French, like us

Southerners, are much more cultured than the rest of the world."

He smiled.

Laurel kissed both her mother and her sister, and then they were in the car heading back to Atlanta.

"Would you like me to put the top up?" she asked.

Christian shook his head. "No, I like the air." He looked at her. "Steamy Georgia air," he said, remembering last night.

She looked at him, laughing. The wind was in her hair; she looked as fresh as springtime, beautiful and desirable. And suddenly Christian wanted to feel the coolness of her cheek against his, the spill of her hair against his throat. He wanted to touch her, wanted it so much that he almost said, "Pull off the road so that I can kiss you."

But he didn't. Instead he looked straight ahead, his eyes on the road, and tried not to think how she would feel in his arms.

Chapter Two

When she turned the car over to the parking valet, Christian asked, out of politeness he told himself, if she would like to have a drink in the bar.

"I don't think so." Laurel looked at her watch. "It's late and you have a breakfast meeting in the morning."

"With your Mr. Dorset," he said.

Her Mr. Dorset? Though she worked for Eli Dorset, she had never thought of him as being "her" Mr. Dorset. He had stolen her away from the Storz-Branda Advertising Agency four years ago with the promise of a terrific salary and year-end bonus. The salary really was terrific and last year's bonus had bought her the red convertible.

She loved her job and she liked and respected Eli. She worked hard for him and she was loyal to him.

He'd told her to zero in on Christian Dumond and that was what she had tried to do, what she would continue trying to do. Up to a point. Christian was an intriguing man. She wanted to get to know him, and not just because it was her job.

"How about a stroll instead of a drink?" she suggested now. "The hotel gardens are lovely at night."

A walk in the garden with a woman as attractive as Laurel? On a night like this when the moon was full and the air was soft with promise? Christian hesitated. It wasn't a good idea, yet he found himself saying, "*Très bien,* Laurel."

As she led the way through the lobby he watched her with speculative eyes, liking the sureness of her stride, the easy confidence in the way she smiled and spoke to some of the conference people she knew. And he liked the way she linked her arm through his, as she had last night.

"Rick Veroni, our landscape artist, designed the gardens," she told him as they stepped outside. "That's why we hired him away from the company he was working for at the time. He works for us now on special projects."

They moved farther into the trees, through feathery foliage and flowers, and a night scented with jasmine and gardenia. She belonged here, Christian thought. She was a part of this. In her pale blue dress and with her hair drifting about her shoulders he could almost see her as she might have been two hundred years ago, a Southern lady, strolling in the garden of her plantation. A black woman, like the woman Euphemia, would have trailed after her.

She stopped before a stone fountain that trickled water turned pink by underground lighting. She sat down on the edge of the fountain and trailed her hand, pale white in the moonlight, through the bubbling water.

"It's beautiful," Christian said. But he wasn't looking at the garden, he was looking at her.

"Veroni is the best there is." Laurel smiled a winning smile. "We'd have him do the gardens at the resort in St. Dominique."

"You never give up, do you?" Christian rested one foot on the edge of the fountain. "I know why I was invited to the conference, Laurel. And I know why I'm being wined and dined and shown around town by the best-looking woman in Atlanta." He looked down at her, his expression serious, hard. "But it won't work. I have no interest in having a resort of the kind you want to build on St. Dominique."

A flush colored Laurel's cheeks. "I'll admit that I invited you to lunch today to talk business. And yes, I thought if we got to know each other a little better—"

"How much better?" His face, by the light of the shadowed moon, looked foreign, exotic and angry. His gray eyes were intent on hers.

He moved closer. She could feel the press of his leg against her hip. "How far did you plan to go in your attempt to convince me?" he asked. "A walk in the garden? A few kisses, purely in the line of duty, of course. Then perhaps a nightcap in your room to seal the bargain?"

He gripped her arms and brought her up beside him. "It's true, isn't it? This is why you brought me out here. This is what Eli Dorset is paying you for."

"No!" Laurel pulled away from him, and whirling, ran down the path that led deeper into the labyrinth of dogwood trees and willows. Tears stung her eyes, tears of shame because a part of what he had said was true. The luncheon today had been planned and so had the drive out into the country. But she hadn't planned on going to White Oaks, and once there she'd forgotten all about the proposed resort. It had been pleasant to sit on the wide veranda with him, to watch darkness come, to listen to the call of the cicadas, the chirp of the crickets. With him. That's what had made it special.

He thought that everything that had happened today had been deliberate. But he was wrong; it hadn't been. He had hurt her with his words and by the scorn she had seen in his eyes.

When a twig snapped and she saw him coming toward her under the willows, she said, "Go away," and turned her back.

But he kept on coming and when he reached her he put a hand on her arm. "I'm sorry," he said. "I shouldn't have said what I did."

"No, you shouldn't have."

"Part of it was true though, wasn't it?"

Laurel turned and faced him. "Part of it. Not all."

Tears glistened on her lashes, her mouth looked soft and vulnerable.

With one slender finger he brushed a tear away. "Why are you crying?" he asked. "Because you're angry?"

"Yes. No. I don't know." She looked at him. "I didn't ask you out here tonight to talk about the resort, Christian."

"Why did you ask me out, Laurel?"

"I wanted you to see the gardens. I wanted . . ."

He tilted her chin up so that they were almost eye to eye. "Was this why?" he asked, and kissed her.

The first touch of his lips sent a shock wave through her. She stiffened, surprised, and tried to move away from him. But he wouldn't let her go. His lips were firm against hers. She felt the heat of his breath, the warmth of his mouth. Without conscious thought her lips parted under his and the hands that had tried to push him away rested on his shoulders.

He urged her closer and she could feel the strength of his lean body hard against hers. His mouth became more demanding, more insistent. She murmured a protest. He touched the tip of his tongue to hers and it was as though she had been struck by lightning. She tried again to draw away, but he held her tight against him, and suddenly she began to answer his kiss. Suddenly she was holding him as he held her.

He let her go. Her turquoise eyes were luminous in the moonlight. He saw the slight tremble of her lips, and felt her body warm against his.

"Laurel?" There was a question in the word. A puzzlement. He drew her back into his arms and kissed her with a fierceness and a hunger that weakened her knees.

She clung to him. She whispered his name, "Christian, Christian," against his mouth, and heard an answering moan of desire.

She had never been kissed like this, had never felt her body respond the way it was responding now. She felt weakened by his kisses, pliant and unresisting in his arms. He brought her closer and a strangled sob escaped her lips. Without thought, without shame, she molded her body to his, and heard the breath rasp deep in his throat.

"Mon Dieu!" he whispered. *"Mon Dieu!"* He let her go and held her away from him.

His eyes were hooded with desire. His lips were parted, the breath coming as hard as if he'd run a ten-mile race.

He cupped her face between his hands and kissed her. Once. Then he let her go and without a word turned and strode away.

Laurel did not move from where she stood. She touched the lips that he had kissed and they were trembling, as she trembled. With slow steps she made her way to one of the iron benches along the pathway and sank down onto it.

"Christian," She said. And his name was a whisper in the soft night air.

She thought about him the moment she awakened the next morning, and lay without opening her eyes, trying to recapture the feel of his lips on hers, the warmth of his arms around her.

She was twenty-nine years old. There had been a lot of other kisses on soft summer nights under the same Georgia moon, but none had affected her the way Christian's had. Never before had she felt that sweet fire, never before had she known that hunger, that yearning.

"Christian Dumond," she whispered, warmed by the sound of his name on her lips.

She would see him at the breakfast meeting this morning. And after the meeting she'd steal him away, the way she had yesterday. They'd go for a drive in the country again, toward Athens, where she had gone to school. She would ask the hotel to pack them a lunch. They would find a rolling hill under a stand of trees to have their picnic. And she wouldn't once mention the projected resort.

She bathed, and dressed in a dark green short-sleeved jumpsuit. With a white jacket it would be suitable for the breakfast meeting, and without the jacket it would be fine for a picnic in the country.

When she was ready, Laurel looked at herself in the mirror. She started to brush her hair off her face into the more severe style she usually wore during business hours but, changing her mind, she brushed it out again and let it fall free about her shoulders. Business or not, today was a special day.

It was ten minutes before nine by the time she went down to the lobby and headed toward the private dining room where she was to meet the top brass of Grand Dorset. And Christian. He was the guest, although target might be a better word, she thought as she cut across the lobby.

"Where in hell have you been?" Eli Dorset, his face florid and his mouth pursed with anger, suddenly appeared in front of her, blocking her way. "I tried to call your room, you weren't there."

"I was on my way here." Laurel looked at her watch. It was five minutes before nine. "I don't think I'm late," she said, "but if I am, I'm sorry."

"Where is he?"

"Where is who?"

"Dumond!"

"Christian Dumond?"

"Of course Christian Dumond! Where is he? Where's he gone?"

"He isn't here?"

"No, dammit. He checked out early this morning."

"But..." She was stunned. She didn't know what to say. "Are you sure?" she said at last.

"Of course I'm sure!" He took her arm and led her to a quieter corner of the lobby. "What happened yesterday?"

"Nothing. I..." She tried to gather her thoughts. Christian was gone. He had left without a word. He hadn't even bothered to call her room to tell her that he was leaving. "We...we had lunch," she said, "and then we went for a drive, out to White Oaks. We had dinner with my mother and after dinner we drove back here." Laurel shook her head. "I don't know what happened," she said.

"Did you talk about the resort?"

"Yes, of course."

"What did he say?"

"He seemed set against it."

"It was your job to convince him."

"I know, Eli, but—"

"Call the airport. See if he's booked a flight back to St. Dominique. Let me know. I'll be in the executive dining room."

Laurel looked at his retreating back, too stunned for a moment to move. Christian was gone; he'd left without telling her. Last night... No, she wouldn't think about last night. She couldn't think about it, not now.

She went up to her second-floor office. She wasn't sure which airline flew to St. Dominique. The second one she called did. "Yes," the young woman who answered said. "There was a flight to Miami that left at seven this morning, with a connecting flight to St. Dominique."

"Could you tell me if there was a Mr. Dumond on the passenger list?" Laurel asked.

"No, ma'am, I'm sorry. I can't give out that information."

"I see. Thank you." Laurel put the phone down and stood there for a moment beside her desk. Last night hadn't meant anything, she told herself. It wasn't important. She had to keep telling herself that. It wasn't important.

"You dropped the ball," Eli said when she went back downstairs. "I told you to zero in on Dumond. It was up to you to convince him to let us build the resort."

Hal Ginsburg shot her a sympathetic look, but Nelson Gladstone, who was first vice president, scowled, and Victor Reiger drummed a pencil against the tabletop. "Inexcusable," he muttered. "Inexcusable."

"Gentlemen, I—"

"Did you call the airline?" Eli Dorset cut in.

"Yes."

"Well? Well? Did Dumond fly back to St. Dominique or not?"

"I'm not sure," Laurel said. "They wouldn't give me that information. But there was a flight for Miami leaving at seven this morning. He was probably on it."

"It's the first time in four years you've let me down," Eli said.

Laurel gripped the back of an empty chair. She'd seen Eli this angry before, had even seen him fire a man on the spot, but he'd never been angry at her. "I'm sorry. I did my best," she said. "Dumond doesn't want Grand Dorset to build on his island."

"His island!" Reiger snorted. "He's not the president of the country. He doesn't run things there."

"In this case he does," Eli said. "He's Minister of Trade and Commerce. What he says about tourism goes. Or in this case, it doesn't go." He smacked the table hard with the flat of his hand. "I'm damned if I'm going to take no for an answer. I want that resort on St. Dominique and, by God, I aim to have it."

He turned to Laurel. "I'm disappointed in you," he said. "But I'm going to give you another chance."

Laurel raised one eyebrow.

"You're going to St. Dominique and you're going to convince Dumond to let us build the resort there, or..."

The word hung in the tense air of the meeting room.

"Or?" Laurel said with a lift of her chin.

"Just come back with his okay for a go-ahead." Eli met her gaze with steely-eyed purpose. "I don't care how long it takes, Merritt. I don't care what you have to do, but I want that resort."

"It might be better if I went instead of Miss Merritt," Victor Reiger said.

"I don't think so." Eli shook his head. "You'd go in like gangbusters, Vic, and ruin everything. This needs a woman's touch, and Laurel is the woman."

He turned to her. "You'll leave on Monday morning, same flight Dumond took. Pick up whatever money you need before you go."

A waiter came into the room and handed menus to the men. Eli did not ask Laurel to sit down.

"That will be all," he said, dismissing her. "I'll expect to be kept up to date. Check in when you get there to let me know where you're staying. I'll want a weekly report."

She left the room without speaking, angry at Eli but more angry at herself because she hadn't told him what he could do with his job. She didn't want to go to St. Dominique. She didn't want to see Christian Dumond.

But she would go because it was her job, only because of that.

The following day, Friday, she telephoned the Ministry of Commerce and Trade in St. Dominique. She did not ask to speak to Dumond, instead she spoke to his secretary.

"This is Laurel Merritt of the Grand Dorset Hotels," she said. "I'm calling from Atlanta. Would you please tell Monsieur Dumond whenever he's available that I'm flying in to St. Dominique on Monday?"

"Of course, Mademoiselle Merritt. But Monsieur Dumond is in his office if you wish to speak to him."

"That won't be necessary. Just tell him that I'm coming and that I would like to see him at his convenience. And I'd appreciate it if you could arrange a room for me at one of your beach hotels."

"Of course, Mademoiselle Merritt. I will also arrange for someone to meet your plane."

"That's very nice of you," Laurel said.

"You are sure you don't want to speak to Monsieur Dumond?"

"Quite sure," Laurel said, and hung up.

When the plane circled over St. Dominique she remembered Christian's words: "It is a tropical paradise," he had said. "A foreign land of grace and enchantment and perpetual summer. The sun warms you during the day, the trade winds cool you at night."

She looked down from her plane window to the green island below and saw the endless stretch of white sand beaches, the rise of distant mountains and the dense vivid green of tropical trees.

"It is a mystical island," he had said. "You must visit it sometime."

The plane circled lower and it seemed to Laurel as though she could see clear to the depths of the turquoise-green water, translucent in the noonday sun. Then they were over the island, coming around toward the narrow landing strip.

"Lord God, but I hate landing here," the man next to her said, and she saw that his knuckles gripping the seat were white.

"Sorry," he muttered. "I'm a bit nervous."

"Yes, so am I," Laurel said.

But her nerves weren't because of the narrow landing strip. They were because soon she would be seeing Christian Dumond.

Chapter Three

She was in the line for customs when someone called, "Mademoiselle Merritt!" and when she turned she saw a nice-looking black man pushing his way through the crowd toward her.

"You are Mademoiselle Merritt?" he asked as he drew closer. And when Laurel nodded he spoke, in French too rapid for her to understand, to the customs agents inspecting the passengers' luggage. The man about to open her bags handed them to her, bowed and said, "Enjoy your stay in St. Dominique, *mademoiselle.*"

"I am Jean-Louis Belain, Monsieur Dumond's assistant," the man who had called out to her said. "He asked me to meet you." He smiled a broad, self-assured smile. "And let me assure you, *mademoiselle,* it is a pleasure."

He was a dapper man, well dressed in dark tailored slacks and a white guayabera shirt with a blue silk ascot. Laurel judged him to be older than Christian, in his early forties perhaps. He was of medium height, bearded and quite good-looking. For a black man, her mother would have said.

She told herself that she really hadn't expected Christian to meet her, yet she couldn't help but feel a twinge of disappointment that he hadn't. She wished now that she hadn't come, that somehow she could have begged out of the assignment and let Victor Reiger come in her stead.

She knew so little about Christian. He might very well have a wife and ten children. That made her swallow hard, but she told herself it had nothing to do with her. She was here on business; she would forget the day she and Christian had spent together. She would forget that he had kissed her.

But when they were in the car and Belain said, "Monsieur Dumond was sorry that he could not meet you himself. There was a family matter he had to attend to," her heart dropped all the way down to her toes.

She cleared her throat. "One of his children?" she asked.

"Christian? Heavens no, he's not married." Belain looked at her and grinned. "Nor am I, Mademoiselle Merritt. It was his sister's little boy," he said. "He fell and broke his arm yesterday. The boy and his mother live with Christian's grandmother up in the mountains. Christian drove out as soon as he heard and brought the boy into the hospital here in Port-au-Mer."

It shouldn't have mattered, yet it did. She could not help but feel an overwhelming sense of relief that Christian wasn't married.

The main avenue into the town of Port-au-Mer was lined with stately royal palms, and as they drew closer Laurel saw that the town itself was situated on the crest of rolling hills that ran down to the sea. The office buildings, none more than three stories tall, looked clean and modern, as did the white houses perched upon the hills.

"How lovely," Laurel said. "Everything looks toward the sea."

"It is a law here in St. Dominique that no one may build a house that obstructs another's view," Belain explained. "That way everyone, no matter how humble their dwelling, can have a view of the water."

He turned to smile at Laurel, his gaze warm and lingering, unmindful of the surge of traffic coming toward them until Laurel cried, "Look out!"

Just in time he saw the oncoming van and veered out of the way. *"Fils de pute!"* he shouted, and shook his fist at the other driver. Then, as though nothing had happened, he said, "There is a good hotel in the center of town, but Monsieur Dumond thought you would prefer to be at the beach." He gave her an appraising head-to-toe look. "I trust you brought a swimsuit?"

"Yes, I did." Laurel looked straight ahead of her.

"The building there," he said, indicating a low white building, "is the Ministry of Commerce and Trade where Christian and I work. I'll give you the telephone number so that you can call me." He flashed her a smile. "In case there is anything I can do for you. Anything at all."

They drove on toward the sea, took a narrow beach road, and ahead of her Laurel saw half a dozen small hotels. Belain drove past them until he came to a larger hotel. It stood away from the others, glistening white except for the deep purple bougainvillea that partially covered one wall. All of its balconied rooms overlooked the sea.

When they drove into the circular driveway two bellmen ran out to take Laurel's bags, while Belain, with great flourish, helped her out of the car.

"The Place Royale is the finest hotel in St. Dominique, Mademoiselle Merritt. I'm sure you will like it, but if there is anything that doesn't please you, tell me." He took her arm and led her past the reception desk. "You are already registered," he said as he walked her to a curved stairway. "I myself will show you to your suite. If it is satisfactory, I will send a maid to unpack for you while we have lunch."

She didn't want to have lunch with him but she could think of no graceful way to refuse. He held on to her arm until they reached a door at one end of the carpeted hall, then stood back for one of the bellmen to open it.

"Voilà!" Belain said when the door was opened.

The walls were done in the palest shade of pink. The ten-foot sofa was white, as were the overstuffed chairs and the carved tables. The floor was tiled in shades of gold and white, and one entire wall of the living room was a glass window that overlooked the blue Caribbean Sea. French doors opened out onto the balcony where there were two chaises, a round table and two canvas-backed chairs.

A camellia plant, filled with dozens of pink flowers, stood at one side of the French doors, and on a long table in front of a gilded mirror there was a huge bouquet of red roses. When she saw the small envelope next to the bouquet, Laurel picked it up and opened it.

"Welcome to my island," it read. And it was signed, "Christian."

She ran her finger across his name, then touched the soft petals of a rose.

"The bedroom is through here," Belain said, opening the door and indicating the other room. "The balcony runs the length of both rooms. Room service is excellent, you need only to call any hour of the day or night."

He went on talking, indicating the small but perfectly equipped kitchen, complete with jars of coffee, imported English tea, croissants, assorted jams and jellies, and a basket of fresh fruit.

She had traveled a great deal for Grand Dorset, both in Europe and South America, and while she had seen hotel rooms that equaled these, she had never seen anything better. There was a charm and a warmth here that both pleased and soothed her. And she was determined, regardless of the outcome of her trip, to enjoy the few days she would spend on St. Dominique.

Belain insisted on taking her downstairs for a late lunch. Over cold lobster and a bottle of white wine, he told her about the island. "There are many things to do here, all kinds of water sports of course, sailing, deep-sea fishing, snorkeling out on the reefs. There are

dances at the country club twice a week, native voodoo, all manner of entertainments." He reached across
the table to cover Laurel's hand. "You must allow me
to show you everything."

"Voodoo?" she asked, sliding her hand from under his.

"Of course." He laughed. "We are a black race,
mademoiselle, we still have our native rituals."

He made her uncomfortable. For one thing she was
too interested in Christian to give any other man more
than a passing glance, and for another thing she had
never dated a black man. She wasn't sure whether it
was because none had seriously asked her out or because she would have felt uncomfortable in doing so.
She only knew that she had absolutely no interest in
dating Jean-Louis Belain.

As soon as they had eaten, Laurel excused herself,
saying she was tired from the trip, which was true because she had been up since five that morning.

"I'll take you up to your room," he said.

"That won't be necessary." She thanked him for
meeting her and for lunch, shook hands with him in
the lobby, and before he could object, turned and went
upstairs to her room.

She did not go down to dinner that night, but instead called room service and had her dinner on the
balcony overlooking the sea.

She told herself that she didn't want to go downstairs because she was tired, but knew it was because
she thought Christian might call.

He didn't.

*   *   *

The phone woke Laurel the next morning at eight-thirty. When she answered a sleepy "Hello," Christian said, "Did I wake you? I'm sorry. Shall I call back?"

"No." She pushed herself up against the pillows. "No, it's all right. I'm awake."

"Is everything satisfactory? Is your suite all right?"

"It's lovely. Thank you for the roses."

"You're welcome. Did you have a good flight? You had no trouble with customs?"

"No. Mr. Belain took care of everything."

There was a moment's hesitation on the other end of the line. Tension tightened her stomach and she wished she hadn't stopped smoking.

"I thought perhaps you would like to see the land your company has in mind for the resort."

"Yes, I'd like that."

"I'll come by for you. Shall we say three o'clock?"

"Three is fine."

"Very well, then. Have a nice day."

Have a nice day? Laurel stared at the phone in her hand, then, with more force than was necessary, slammed it down and lay back against the pillows. Okay, she told herself. Face it. The man has absolutely no interest in you. This is strictly business. As soon as you can convince him to let Dorset have the land you'll be on the first plane back to Atlanta.

So he kissed you. Big deal! You had too many glasses of champagne and it went to your head. Steamy night in Georgia. Ha!

She threw back the sheet and padded into the bathroom. He hadn't even asked her to lunch. He could have done that at least, out of professional courtesy if nothing else. But he hadn't; he was making it perfectly clear that their relationship was strictly business.

That was fine with her, she told herself in the shower. Christian Dumond was just a man her boss had told her to zero in on. That's what she'd done. The day they'd spent together meant as little to her as it did to him. And the kiss? Fiddle-dee-dee, as Scarlett would have said. It hadn't been important at all.

She put a bathing suit on and went out to the kitchen to fix coffee, banging the cupboards harder than necessary, scowling while she spread orange marmalade on the fresh croissants. She put the coffee and the croissants on a tray and carried it out to the balcony. And there her anger evaporated.

The sea was a calm cerulean blue. Puffs of white clouds floated in the clear sky. Tall palms and frangipani trees, their blossoms bright red in the sunlight, lined the path down to the beach. Thatched umbrellalike shelters were spaced along the sand; yellow chaises surrounded the swimming pool where gardenias floated. Sailboats, their sails stiffened by an offshore breeze, skimmed over the sea. It was the most breathlessly beautiful day she had ever seen.

As soon as she finished breakfast she put a terrycloth robe over her swimsuit and went down to the beach. A young man set up a chaise for her in the shade of one of the thatched shelters. She took off her robe, rubbed suntan lotion over her face and arms, and decided she'd take a walk along the beach before she settled down.

The tide was up and the water that splashed at her feet was warm. There were few tourists out and only now and then did she pass anyone. The other hotels she saw were smaller, more like family-owned pensions. She wondered if a resort like the one Grand Dorset wanted to build would bring more tourists to St. Dominique. And if it did, she thought uncomfortably, would it ruin this tropical paradise?

She walked until she felt her skin beginning to burn, then turned toward the hotel. She debated about whether to go in the pool or the sea, and decided on the sea. The water was warm, with only the barest ripple of waves. She swam straight out, then turned onto her back and looked up at the sky. It was so quiet, the only sound the gentle slap of the waves and the occasional cry of a gull. Floating there, rocked in the cradle of the water, all of the tension and the anger she'd felt earlier seemed to seep out of her pores, and she allowed herself to think about Christian. She remembered the touch of his lips on hers and the way she had responded. What she had felt had been an honest emotion; she would not diminish it by pretending that it didn't matter. She could not help it if her feelings were not reciprocated, but she would not be sorry that Christian had kissed her.

When at last Laurel came out of the water she went to the chaise under the thatched shelter and stretched out, so relaxed that it felt as though her bones had melted. She dozed, and when she awoke she ordered a sandwich and a cool drink and looked out at the sea while she had her lunch.

Upstairs she showered and washed her hair. In a little while she would see Christian again. And it would be all right, for, whatever happened, she would not be sorry that she had come to St. Dominique. Or that in a way she could not explain something important had happened in her life. She would not be sorry that it had.

He had told himself that what had happened in Atlanta was of little or no importance. He had kissed a beautiful woman in a moonlit garden. It had been a pleasant experience, nothing more. He had kissed other women in other gardens; there had been nothing special about Laurel Merritt.

Yet when Christian got out of his car in front of the Place Royale he realized that the palms of his hands were damp and that his mouth was dry. It's the heat, he told himself. The dryness of the air. I should have arranged to show her the land in the morning when it was cool.

He looked at his watch; it was five minutes before three. He dried his damp palms on the sides of his trousers and went into the lobby—just as she started down the curved staircase.

She had on a simple white summer dress and white sandals. Her hair was soft about her face, and there were yellow daisy earrings in her ears.

She reached the bottom of the stairs. "Hello," she said, and offered her hand.

He took it. For a moment he couldn't speak. And when he did he said, "Your nose is sunburned."

"I stayed out on the beach too long. I couldn't help it. It's so beautiful here."

"Yes, it is." He couldn't seem to let go of her hand.

"I'm anxious to see more of your island."

He took a deep breath and releasing her, said, "My car is right outside."

It was a small white sports car. The top was down. The attendant helped her in and closed the door after her.

They didn't speak as Christian started off, he because he could not think of anything to say, Laurel because it was enough to be with him again.

They drove along the beach. There was a breeze and at last he said, "You don't mind the wind?"

Laurel shook her head. "I love it," she said. "I love the smell of the sea."

He glanced at her, and quickly away.

They began to climb higher into the mountains and the scenery changed to a tropical lushness of technicolor beauty. Palms of every variety lined the road, along with papaya and mango trees heavy with fruit. In another place there was a thickness of fern, bright green in the shaded light, and farther on a jungle of wild orchids, blooming like colorful butterflies in shades of yellow tinged with specks of brown, purple, dark orange and white.

Laurel leaned back, her head against the smooth leather seat, her body relaxed, breathing in the beauty all around her. She wanted to touch Christian's hand, to tell him what the sharing of this beauty meant to her, but she did not. It was enough to be with him again.

At last they started the winding descent down toward the sea. The vegetation became heavier, thicker. Below she could see the Caribbean, sparkling blue-green in the afternoon sun. Christian slowed the car and she saw before her a place more beautiful than any she had ever seen, a rolling green plain of land over-looking the sea. The vegetation here was full and thick, the palms tall and stately sentinels constructed by nature to guard this most beautiful of places.

Christian parked under a banyan tree. Without looking at her he said, "This is where your company wants to build the resort."

Laurel looked about her in wonder. Never had she seen a more perfect location. Behind them there was the rise of mountains, in front of them the sea. "It's perfect," she said. "I can see the way it would be, the hotel overlooking the Caribbean, terraces down to the sea, a tennis court, a—"

"No!" His voice was vehement, angry because he had thought that if he brought her here she would un-derstand. But she didn't. All she could see was the possibility of the kind of a resort her company wanted to build.

He got out of the car. "Come," he said, and when Laurel gave him her hand he brought her up beside him. "Do you see that place there under the trees?" he asked, indicating a section of land that lay just be-neath the fall of the mountain. "That's a burial ground. It's very old, more than three hundred years most likely. Carib Indians are buried there, and so are the blacks who were brought to St. Dominique to work as slaves in the sugarcane fields."

He let go of her hand and moved closer to the place he was talking about. "So many of them died," he said, almost to himself. "From disease, from over-work, from being brutalized." He looked at Laurel. "It was the same in your country," he said. "In your South."

Intellectually she knew it was true. Slaves *had* been treated badly. But that wasn't what the rest of her family believed. They thought maybe there were exceptions, those few cases of brutal treatment that the nicer families whispered about, but for the most part the Southern slaves had been treated well. Her mother had told her so.

"Your great-great-granddaddy, James Carlton Merritt, had over thirty coloreds working in the fields and in the house," Darcie Ann had said. "And believe me, honey, they were a whole lot happier than the coloreds are today. They had enough to eat and a roof over their heads, and they didn't have to worry about making any decision. James Carlton made sure of that."

"They weren't given an opportunity to make any decisions," Laurel had argued. "They had no rights, everything was decided for them."

"As well it should have been." With a shake of her head because Laurel didn't seem to grasp her meaning, Darcie Ann said, "We're talking about black people, darlin'. Believe me, they were happy to have somebody do the thinking for them."

Laurel had given up trying to argue with her mother, or with Virgie for that matter. Theirs was a mind-set she didn't understand. She could have argued until she turned blue and nothing would have changed. But most people weren't like that anymore. The civil rights movement had made people aware that change was needed. Sometimes change came too slowly, but Laurel believed it did occur.

She respected Christian for his feelings about the people who had died here, and in a gentle voice she said, "That portion of the land could be fenced off. There could be a plaque explaining what it was, what it meant to the descendants of the men and women who are buried there."

But Christian shook his head. "This is sacred land," he said. "We don't want a modern hotel. The land belongs to the spirits of those who died here."

Laurel wanted to understand, but there was in her that sense of realism, of business logic that could not let go without a fight.

"The land belongs to the spirits?" She smiled. "Come on, Christian, you're an educated man. Surely you don't believe that."

"But I do believe it, Laurel, and so do most of the St. Dominicans."

She looked up at him, about to make a joking remark, but she was stopped by the expression on his face. The very first time she had seen him she had been struck by a hint of something primeval about him, something in his eyes, in the line of his body that reminded her of a jungle animal, a leopard, she thought now, or a panther. Yes, that was it, that's what he was like, a strong, sleek panther.

For a reason she could not explain, that frightened even as it excited her.

His face, shadowed by the fading light of the afternoon sun, was pensive, thoughtful. "Once a year the people of St. Dominique come here to honor the memory of those who came before them," he said. "It's primitive celebration, ritualistic, African. Part Christian, part voodoo, and part of the ancient religion the early Africans brought with them when they came to St. Dominique."

His voice changed as he spoke and his face became remote, and there was in his eyes an expression Laurel had not seen before. It was something she did not understand.

"It's a ceremony of remembrance," he went on. "A reaching out to those who suffered and died here on this island. They cry out to the African homeland. 'Take me back to the land of my forefathers,' they call into the darkness of the night. 'Take me back to where I belong.'"

He looked at Laurel, but she thought that he did not really see her. "Civilization is forgotten," he said. "There is a singing of a type you could not understand, and tribal dances to the beat of ancient drums. It's wild and it's wonderful. It's..." He shook his head as though clearing it. "I'm sorry," he murmured. "I've said too much."

Laurel put her hand on his arm. "No," she said. "I want to hear. I want to understand."

"To understand?" He looked at her. "You can never understand."

"I can try," she said.

"Can you?" He looked at her intently, his eyes searching hers. Her gaze didn't waver. Then abruptly he said, "Come, let's go closer to the edge," and taking her hand, he led her to the very edge of the cliff overlooking the sea.

"Tell me more," she said. "Tell me more about when the French came."

"They brought slaves from Africa to work in the sugarcane fields," Christian said. "Eventually their French blood mixed with the African and today most St. Dominicans are black or mulatto. There are also the white descendants of the French settlers and they are the ones who pretty much control the economy and hold most of the key government positions."

"Like you and your family," Laurel said.

A muscle jumped in Christian's jaw. "Laurel," he said. "There is something I—"

"Look!" she cried. "Oh, Christian, look!" And he turned to see a school of dolphins leaping from the water, their bodies silvered and translucent, the sea sluicing off them like drops of sparkling gold in the last rays of the setting sun.

Her hand tightened around his. "Have you ever seen anything so beautiful?" she whispered.

He looked at the dolphins and then he looked at her. Her eyes were shining, and her hair was soft about her face. He lay his hand upon her head and she turned to look at him.

Her expression changed. Her lips parted, her eyes questioned. A small sigh escaped her lips, and suddenly she was in his arms and he was kissing her the way he had wanted to kiss her since that moment when she had come down the curving staircase. He kissed her with all of the longing he had held in check since that magical night in the garden in Atlanta. Kissed her with hunger and passion, and with a sense of being one with another that he had never known before.

She felt his hunger and knew his passion. She whispered his name against his lips and her arms came up around his shoulders to hold him as he held her. She felt his power and his strength, and rejoiced in it.

The kiss ended. He held her a little away from him but he did not let her go. With their arms around each other they watched the sun slowly disappear into the blue-green waters of the Caribbean.

Chapter Four

They had dinner at a restaurant in the mountains, in a junglelike setting, surrounded by all manner of tropical trees and foliage. Music from inside the restaurant mingled with the cry of night birds and wild animals.

Was there a panther among the animals? Laurel wondered. A splendid beast that stalked through the brush, sleek and strong and powerful, yellow eyes shining in the darkness, seeking . . . What? She smiled a secret smile because she knew she was being fanciful, and because that was how she thought of Christian. He, too, was a splendid animal, exotic and dangerous, by far the most attractive man she had ever met.

A little while ago he had kissed her. In a way she could not explain it had seemed to her that all of her life she had been waiting for that one perfect moment, and at last it had come, there in Christian's arms. She had felt a wondrous sense of belonging and as she stood looking out at the sea with him, she had experienced a gladness of heart that she felt this emotion, this sense of rightness in being with Christian.

She had not voiced any of what she was feeling, nor had he. When they drove away and started the climb into the mountains again she had longed for a word from him, and if not a word, then the touch of his hand, a gesture, a look that would tell her that he, too, had felt a bonding of heart and of spirit.

But he had remained silent, with both hands on the wheel, staring straight ahead.

When they were seated at a candlelit table on the terrace he ordered a bottle of champagne, and when the waiter filled their glasses Christian touched his to hers and said, "To your visit here in St. Dominique, Laurel." For just a moment his gaze met hers across the table.

In the flickering candlelight she saw his eyes soften. He seemed about to speak, then with an almost imperceptible shake of his head said, "I'll order for us, some island dishes, if that's all right with you."

"Of course," she said.

They had a pepper-pot soup made from Indian kale, okra and finely chopped meat. It was followed by conch fritters, roasted breadfruit and chicken garnished with crayfish. There were petit fours for dessert, and rich Jamaican coffee.

He had been to this particular restaurant many times before, sometimes on business, sometimes with other women. But never had he enjoyed an evening more. Laurel was a lovely companion. Her enthusiasm for the food had both amused and pleased him. She'd tasted the pepper-pot soup, smiled, and had eaten it all. When she started on the chicken she'd sighed in contentment. She had eaten three petits fours with murmured purrs of pleasure. On the last one she'd left a bit of chocolate at the corner of her mouth and as her tongue had appeared to lick it off he'd had an overwhelming desire to say, "No, wait, let me do it."

He liked her enthusiasm for food, and suddenly he remembered a mystery writer who had once said that a woman's appetite for food was indicative of her appetite for sex. He looked at Laurel gazing longingly at the last petit four and found himself wondering if that was true.

She smiled at him from across the table. Her turquoise eyes were slumberous with the satisfaction of a good meal, her mouth softly relaxed.

"Laurel?"

She stirred, moving her body in a lazy, graceful way, and he thought, yes, she is a sexual woman, and knew how it would be when finally they made love. His muscles tightened. No, he told himself, I won't think about that. I won't think about the way it could be because it cannot be. But the need to hold her was strong and so he said, "Would you like to dance?"

"Mmm." She smiled and held her hand out to him. It was cool in his, soft, fragile. He rubbed his thumb across her palm, then brought her up beside him. She looked at him, lips slightly parted, waiting. But he would not allow himself to yield to all that he was feeling.

He led her inside to a room where a small orchestra played, and at last he took her in his arms. Her hair brushed his cheek. He caught again the scent of her perfume, and felt the soft crush of her breasts against his chest, the line of her hip against his. It was heaven and it was hell to hold her like this. He knew that he should say, "It's late. Perhaps we should start back to the city," but he did not.

They danced without speaking, fingers intertwined, communicating by the movement of their bodies, the slight pressure of his hand against the small of her back. They were unaware of other couples, one with the music and with each other, not wanting it to end.

When it did, when the music stopped and the other couples moved away, they stayed for a moment, still locked in each other's arms in one darkened corner of the dance floor. Laurel looked up at him, still lost in the music, reluctant to move out of the warmth of his embrace.

"It's late," he said.

"Yes."

And still they did not move.

He said her name, "Laurel," then with a shake of his head he stepped away from her.

"Why did you leave?" she asked.

"What?" he said, not understanding.

"Why did you leave Atlanta without telling me?"

"I had to," he said. "Something came up. Business. I had to leave."

"But there was a breakfast meeting you were supposed to attend. You weren't there." She shook her head. "You should have told me you were leaving."

"As a professional courtesy?"

Her eyes were steady, unwavering. "No," she said, "not because of professional courtesy."

"There was a reason," he said.

She shook her head. "I don't understand."

"I know you don't." He took her hand. "Come," he said, and led her away from that darkened corner of the dance floor.

There was so much about Christian she didn't understand. There were times when he looked at her that she saw warmth and desire in his eyes. At other times a remoteness that chilled her. What is it? she wanted to ask. Why do you pull away from me?

Jean-Louis had said that Christian wasn't married. What was it, then? Did he have a mistress? A long-term relationship that meant a great deal to him? And if he did, then what was this . . . this *something* that happened whenever they were together?

The night was soft and still. He drove without speaking. The road was dark, narrow and winding. There was no guardrail to prevent a skidding car from falling the almost three thousand feet to the sea below. Yet Laurel was not afraid; she knew she was safe with him.

By the dim dashboard light she studied the planes and the hollows of his face, the high forehead, the sharp cheekbones, the full and sensuous lips. The first time she had seen him she had thought him the most attractive man she had ever seen. And it was true, for while not classically handsome, there was something so special about him, something so sensuously magnetic that she felt a sense of excitement every time she looked at him.

A sharp curve brought her closer. She put her hand on his thigh. When she did she felt his muscles tighten against her palm, but she did take her hand away.

They came to a turnoff, no more than a rutted path hidden from the road by an overhang of trees. He slowed the car, hesitated, and turned into it. He didn't speak when he stopped the car, nor did she. But when he put his arm around her shoulder she rested her head against it and, closing her eyes, breathed in the scent of the jungle and of the sea below.

She could feel the tenseness of his body, and she waited, her heart beating hard against her ribs, until with a slight pressure of his fingers against her shoulder he brought her into his arms.

"Laurel." He breathed her name against her hair, and kissed her with a passion he could no longer hold in check. Her hands crept up around his neck to caress his skin, to touch the fine hairs that grew there.

The kiss deepened. He touched his tongue to hers and she shivered but did not draw away. Again, as he had when they danced, he felt the press of her breasts against his chest, but now he cupped her there, and felt her, soft and warm through the fabric of her dress. She moaned into his mouth and the sound of it ran like a shock wave through him, tightening his body, sending the blood pounding through his veins.

He had to stop, had to let her go, and yet... Her lips were so incredibly soft; her mouth tasted like warm honey. He wanted to make love to her, with her. He wanted to do everything with her he had ever wanted to do with a woman. *Mon Dieu,* he wanted...

"Christian." A whispered plea against his lips as her arms tightened around him. "Christian."

He kissed her throat and felt the frantic beat of her pulse against his lips. Her hands slipped down over his shoulders. She struggled with the buttons of his shirt and when she had opened them she slipped her hand inside and began to run her palm against the curly thatch of his chest hair. His skin burned where she touched him. He groaned aloud, seeking her mouth, kissing her with a ferocity that left them both breathless.

He had to stop. *Mon Dieu,* if he did not . . . He held Laurel away from him. Her eyelids were heavy, her lips full and trembling from his kisses. He cupped her breasts again and ran his thumb once over the tips, heard her indrawn breath, and knew that he could take her here in this jungle place, here in the darkness of the night, on the jungle floor. He could . . . A shudder ran through him. He let her go and clamped both hands hard on the steering wheel.

"What . . . ?" She looked dazed. "What is it?"

"Very likely the champagne." He forced a smile. "I'm afraid I've been behaving badly. I'm sorry."

Laurel stared at him. Shame burned her cheeks; she felt as though she had been slapped.

He started the car and slowly backed onto the road. He knew that he had hurt her and that this wasn't her fault, it was his. He should have known better than to have kissed her again. But ever since he had left Atlanta . . . No, he thought, not left, fled. Like the Southern troops fleeing General Sherman, he had run for his life. Because her kisses had stirred him as no other kisses ever had. Because that night in the garden he had wanted her as badly as he did now. And because there was no way on God's green earth that it could ever work out between them.

They didn't speak all the way back to Port-au-Mer. Laurel sat as far over on her side of the car as she could, silent, withdrawn. Hurting.

Christian stopped at the entrance of the hotel. She got out of the car before he could assist her, but he opened his door and came around the car to put a detaining hand on her arm. "We need to talk about this," he said.

She wouldn't look at him. "I want to go in," she said. "I'm very tired."

He took a deep breath. "I'll call you."

"Good night," she said, and, turning away, went quickly into the hotel.

He took a step toward the hotel, then stopped and hurried around to his side of the car. And drove away fast, burning rubber like a rejected teenager on his first date.

Shame cut into her like a blunted knife. She went to sleep with it, she awoke in the night with it. Christian had only meant to kiss her; the local guide giving the lady tourist the full treatment: dinner, dancing and the obligatory moonlight kiss. She had responded like a love-starved spinster, ready and willing, and oh, so eager to make love.

She would never, ever, for as long as she lived, forget that moment when he had held her away from him and said that he was sorry, that perhaps he'd had too much champagne. She would have left St. Dominique that same night if it hadn't been for her job.

When the phone rang the next morning she let it ring, afraid that it was Christian. But when finally she answered it wasn't Christian, it was Eli Dorset.

"How's it going?" he asked.

"All right." She took a deep breath and tried to force herself to relax. "Yesterday, Mr. Dumond showed me the land you want to buy."

"And?"

"It's a beautiful place."

"Damn right. Told you so, didn't I? So what happened?"

"He still doesn't want the resort built there."

"Offer him more money."

"I don't think it's a matter of money, Eli."

"Everything's a matter of money. Up the ante."

"How high do you want to go?"

"Double the offer to six."

"Six million? That's a lot of money."

"But think what we'll make once the resort's been built. When are you going to see Dumond again?"

"I'm not sure."

"Make it soon." Eli's voice hardened. "I want that resort, Laurel. If I don't get it..." The threatening words hung in the air. "If you can't do the job, I'll find somebody who can."

Her hands were shaking when she put the receiver down. She went out onto the balcony and, grasping the railing, stood looking out at the azure sea. If Christian didn't call her, she would have to call him. She didn't think she could do that.

He didn't call, but later that afternoon Jean-Louis Belain did.

"Monsieur Dumond has suggested that I show you around the island," he said. "Although he objects to letting your company have the site of land they want, there are other places we might consider selling. Are you free tomorrow morning?"

"Yes, I'm free."

"Shall we say ten o'clock?"

"Ten is fine."

"Is everything all right? Is there anything I can do for you?"

"No, Mr. Belain, but thank you."

"How about dinner tonight? I know a charming little place up in the mountains—"

"No!" she said, more sharply than she had intended. Then, "I'm sorry, Mr. Belain. Thank you very much for asking but I'm afraid I've had a bit too much sun today and I'm a little tired. I'm going to have a light dinner in my room and go to bed early."

"Perhaps I could join you." He chuckled. "For dinner, I mean."

"I know what you mean," she said. "But I'm afraid not."

He gave an exaggerated sigh. "Then I will see you in the morning, *non?* Sleep well, *mademoiselle.*"

Laurel replaced the phone. Christian had asked Belain to call. She wondered if he had also asked the other man to take her to dinner—to that same restaurant in the mountains.

She went to the balcony and stared out at the tranquil sea. In the setting sun the sky caught fire, sending streaks of brilliant red into the fading blue, that softened first to pink, then to a darkening gold, and finally, as silently as a lover's kiss, to darkness.

Sleep was a long time coming that night, but it came with disturbing dreams. She was alone on a long and perfect stretch of white sand beach. The sea was dead calm, but as she watched, a wave began to form. It grew bigger as it moved toward the shore, twenty feet high, thirty... Fear choked her. She tried to run. The wave came closer. She felt the spray on her face and cried out for help, but there was no one to hear. The wave was upon her. It swept her up and carried her away...

Away to an exotically beautiful garden. She wandered along a flower-lined path until at last she came to a secluded place amid a thickness of fern and sheltering trees. She lay upon soft green grass. The sun warmed her naked body and she felt more at peace, and more alive, than she ever had before.

There was a movement in the underbrush. She closed her eyes, scarcely daring to breathe, and felt the softness of fur brush against her body, sleek and smooth against her skin. She felt his breath against her cheek, but, unafraid, she neither opened her eyes nor moved away. Instead she held out her arms to welcome him into her embrace.

"Darling," she whispered. "Oh, darling."

It was drizzling when Belain picked up Laurel in front of the hotel. "I'm sorry about the weather," he said when he helped her into the car. "It's only a summer shower, it will stop soon."

The sky was a threatening gray, darkened with clouds that scudded overhead. They drove along the beach, and the sea, like the clouds, was a flat and threatening gray. Laurel thought of the dream she'd had and looked away from the water to the rise of mountains in the distance.

Five miles out of the city, Belain—"Call me Jean-Louis," he had said, squeezing her knee—stopped the car and gestured to a piece of land some three hundred yards from the sea.

"I'm sorry it's still raining," he said, "but you can see for yourself what a fine piece of property it is."

"How far does the land extend?" Laurel asked.

"All the way to that forest of trees." He indicated a stand of coconut palms. "It covers an area of almost seven acres, *mademoiselle,* more than enough to build the kind of resort Dorset is so famous for."

It was a beautiful piece of land, close to the sea, and the distance from the city was good. But it could not compare to the land she had seen with Christian. Still, she wrote down the location, the size and the price, and a general description of the area.

Next Jean-Louis took her to a place that was too far from the beach. "You could compensate for that with swimming pools," he said. "And perhaps with a minibus or a horse-drawn carriage to shuttle your guests back and forth to the beach."

"Perhaps," Laurel said, and though she knew it would not do, she made a note of it.

Over lunch at a seaside restaurant, Belain asked her if she would have dinner with him that evening. She refused, making the excuse that she had to stay in because her boss had said he would call and she had no idea when.

"Then we will dine in your suite," he said.

"I don't think so."

"But why, *ma chère* Laurel? A woman as lovely as you should not spend her evenings alone." He raised an eyebrow. "Perhaps you have met someone at the hotel, or perhaps you have been occupying your time with Monsieur Dumond?"

Laurel picked up her purse. "And perhaps you had better take me back to my hotel, Mr. Belain."

He slapped a hand to his forehead. *"Mon Dieu!"* he exclaimed. "I have offended you. Believe me, *mademoiselle,* I did not mean to. It was only a joke, *n'est-ce pas?"*

When they left the restaurant, Belain took the road that led up into the mountains. "There is a most beautiful piece of land that you must see," he told Laurel. "It is very high up with a perfect view of the Caribbean. I'm sure you will like it."

He drove very fast, accelerating on the winding curves, gesturing with one hand, taking his eyes off the road to look at Laurel when he spoke.

"Be careful," she said once, but he only laughed.

"I have driven this road hundreds of times," he said. "I know it as well as I know my mother's face." He patted her leg. "Do not worry, my dear Laurel, you are in my most capable hands."

It began to rain again just before they reached the place that he wanted to show her.

"Bad luck," he said, then with a grin added, "We will have to come back tomorrow, no?"

No, Laurel thought. Good God, no! And in as calm a voice as she could manage she said, "The rain seems to be getting worse, Mr. Belain. I really think we should be starting back."

"Very well, Laurel. But we will come again, yes?"

He started back down the mountain road. Rain beat against the windows, so hard that she could barely see. When Belain made no attempt to slow down, she said, "You're going too fast. I'd be more comfortable if you slowed down a bit."

"Whatever you say, *ma chère.*" He squeezed her knee, and left his hand there.

"Please," Laurel said. But when she tried to remove his hand he slid it farther up her thigh.

"Your skin is so smooth," he murmured. "Are you as soft as this all over?"

"Mr. Belain!" She started to move away from him, but when she did he laughed, and tightened his hand around her leg.

She dug her nails into the back of his hand and he said, "You are a little wildcat, yes? *Très bien,* that is the way I like my women." He gave her leg another caress.

"Don't!" She tried to pry his fingers loose. "Please," she said. "Don't do this, don't..." The car careered close to the edge of the road, throwing her hard against the door. Through the rain she saw the earth falling away to the drop below. Forcing herself to speak more calmly, she said, "Please be careful. This road is dangerous."

Belain laughed and turned to look at her. "I could drive it in my sleep. I—"

The sound of a horn cut through the rain. Belain saw the headlights of a car coming toward them. Too late.

Laurel screamed and tried to brace herself, one hand against the dashboard, the other on the roof of the car. Belain swerved and she was thrown violently against him, then slammed against her door. Their car veered straight to the edge where there was no guardrail. Cursing, Belain stamped on the brake, and the car hovered there on the brink of the curve, right wheels hanging over the edge of the nothingness that lay two thousand feet below.

Too terrified to move, too mute with fear to cry out, Laurel froze.

Belain clutched the wheel, then gunned the car back onto the road. "There, you see?" He forced a laugh. "We're all right now, we..."

The car skidded. His foot reached for the brake but hit the gas. The rock face of the mountain loomed hard in front of them. The car hurtled straight toward it.

Laurel screamed once more.

But her scream was lost in the terrible sound of tearing metal and breaking glass.

Then, except for the rain and one small feeble cry before the darkness closed in about her, there was only silence.

Chapter Five

Hush little baby, don't you cry
Daddy's gonna sing you a lullaby...

Laurel buried her face against his jacket, over-
whelmed by the miracle of being with him again, and
breathed in the scent of old leather, of bourbon and
pipe tobacco. So dearly familiar, a part of her childhood.

"You went away," she whispered.

"But you'll always be my little girl."

"I missed you, Daddy. Can I come with you now?"

"Not now, baby. Someday..."

"Laurel!" a voice called out to her.

"Wait for me, Daddy. Wait... Oh, please..."

He kissed her forehead, but when she reached out
for him he shook his head and began to fade, then

vanished into a misty nothingness until she could no longer see him.

"Come back," she whispered. "Oh, Daddy, come back."

"She's coming around," a voice said. "I think she's going to make it."

Make what? She didn't understand. Where had her father gone? She wanted to open her eyes but it hurt too much to try. Everything hurt, even the prick of a needle in her arm.

A warm hand gripped hers. She said, "Don't leave me," then darkness came again.

Sunshine awakened her. She opened her eyes and when she did she saw Christian beside her bed.

She tried to sit up but pain cut through her and she sank back onto the pillows. "Where am I?" she managed to ask.

"You're in a hospital in Port-au-Mer. There was an accident. You were hurt."

"An accident?" She tried to remember. Rain. Yes, she remembered the rain. And the narrow road, the mountains. "He told me to call him Jean-Louis," she whispered, still in that half world between wakefulness and sleep. "He had his hand on me and I didn't want him to..." She looked up at Christian, fear in her eyes. "Something happened, but I don't...I don't remember."

The doctor had said that she might not, that often a concussion as severe as the one she'd had caused temporary amnesia. "It will all come back to her in a few days," the doctor had assured Christian. "She's out of danger now, but she'll have to be watched for a week or two at the very least."

Christian took her hand. "It's all right," he said reassuringly. "You're safe, Laurel. That's all that matters now."

"But why can't I remember? What's wrong with me?"

"You had a concussion. You were unconscious." He squeezed her hand. "But you're going to be all right, Laurel. In a few days you'll be fine."

The police had called him right after the accident. He'd been about to leave the office and when the phone rang he'd said to his secretary, "If that's for me, say I've already left." She'd nodded, but when she answered the phone she called out, "Monsieur Dumond! It's the police. There's been an accident. It's Monsieur Belain. Miss Merritt was with him."

He barely remembered taking the phone from her hand, talking to the police or driving to the hospital. He'd arrived just as they were bringing Laurel in. She had been unconscious, her face dead white except for the blood.

The doctors had made him wait while they examined her. They wiped the blood away. They bandaged her head and wheeled her past him into the X-ray room.

"There are no broken bones," a doctor came to tell him. "Her arms were cut by the broken glass and she's terribly bruised. She has a bad concussion. We'll have to watch her very carefully for the next few days."

"Get round-the-clock nurses," Christian said. "And I want a neurosurgeon."

The doctor had nodded. "I've already telephoned a colleague of mine in Miami. He's flying in tonight."

They'd taken Laurel to a private room and he had gone with her. She had been unconscious for all of that day and night and the following day. He'd never been more afraid. He had never prayed harder.

There had been a moment when they had almost lost her. He had seen it in the doctor's eyes, had heard it in his voice when he said, "The longer she's unconscious the more dangerous it is, Monsieur Dumond."

Laurel had called for her father, and she'd hummed a song he had never heard. He'd held her hand, gripping it hard. And he'd called out to her, "Laurel! Laurel, wake up!"

And finally, almost thirty hours after the accident, she had opened her eyes.

"I spoke with Eli Dorset but I haven't called your mother," Christian said to her now. "Do you want me to?"

"No." She shook her head, and winced. "No, don't. She can't cope with things like this."

"Can I get you anything?"

"Some water, please."

He eased her off the pillow a little. She hissed with pain and closed her eyes. "I hurt," she whispered, and took a sip of water.

"Easy," he said gently. "Easy."

She looked up at him. "I'm glad you're here," she said, and closed her eyes.

Every time she opened them Christian was there beside her. And though there was a nurse, it was Christian who held fruit juice to her lips, who bathed her face and soothed her when the pain came. And once when she was almost asleep she felt the touch of his lips against her cheek.

Every day there were fresh flowers in her room: red roses, orchids, pink camellias floating in a silver bowl. When she was in pain or grew restless he read to her, sometimes in English and sometimes in a French she barely understood but loved to hear because it soothed and comforted her. As he did.

She did not question why he was here; it was enough that he was.

By the end of the week the doctor who had first attended her said, "You're well enough to leave the hospital. You're staying at the Place Royale, aren't you?"

"Yes, Doctor."

He frowned. "I'd like it better if you had someone with you. Perhaps one of the nurses—"

"But I'm all right now," Laurel protested.

"You might think about sending for your mother."

But Laurel shook her head. "I don't want to do that," she said.

"Very well. But you must rest as much as you can. Send down for your meals, and take it easy. In another week you'll be back on your feet again."

The following morning at eleven, Christian arrived. "I stopped by the hotel and packed a bag for you," he said. "You'll need something to wear. The clothes you were wearing at the time of the accident were torn, bloody...." He stopped and ran a hand across his face. "I'll wait outside while the nurse helps you change," he said.

They took her out to his car in a wheelchair. He helped her in. "All right?" he asked.

"I'm fine, Christian." She took a deep breath and looked around. The sky was blue, the air was fresh. "It's awfully nice to be outside again," she said. "I'm going to enjoy being back at the hotel."

"You're not going back to the hotel. I'm taking you home with me."

"You're taking me...?" Laurel looked at him, surprised. "But you can't do that."

"Of course I can." He smiled. "I'm kidnapping you, Mademoiselle Merritt, and I'm afraid there isn't anything you can do about it."

"I could yell for the *gendarmes.*"

"But you won't."

"No," she said. "I won't."

She didn't know why he was taking her to his home, nor did she know why he had spent almost every minute of this past week at her bedside. She hadn't questioned, she had only been content that he was with her. Now she didn't question his reason for taking her home with him.

He drove carefully, but when a car coming from the other direction was passed by a car that cut in too sharply and veered toward them, she screamed and tried to shrink back against the leather seat. Shock waves of terror ran through her. She clutched at Christian's arm and stamped both feet hard down on the floor of the car as though trying to stop it.

The other car swept past, and when it did Christian pulled to the side of the road. He put an arm around her shoulder, and felt her trembling. "Take it easy, *ma chère,*" he said. "I'm not going to let anything hurt you."

"The accident..." She shuddered against him. "I remember. The car skidded. We smashed...we smashed into the mountain." She looked up at him. "Monsieur Belain," she said. "Is he all right? Was he hurt?"

"Not as badly as you were." Christian tightened his arm around her. "You've had a frightening experience," he said gently. "It's going to take you a while to get over it, Laurel."

Yes, she thought, it will. For though until now she had not really remembered the accident, she remembered the fear. Again and again in those odd moments between sleep and wakefulness she relived that feeling of terror. And now, still in the throes of that terror, she relived that moment the car crashed into the mountain, and heard again that frightening sound of twisted metal and breaking glass.

Christian put his hand on the back of her head and drew her closer. Unmindful of the cars that passed, he held her until the panic ebbed and the tension left her body.

"Better?" he said at last.

Laurel nodded, and moved away from the comfort of his embrace.

In a little while he turned off the main highway onto a private road lined with royal palms and brilliantly flowered frangipani trees. Ahead Laurel saw the blue Caribbean, and his home, standing on a rise of land surrounded by a green lawn and a lushness of tropical plants and flowers, stark white against the panorama of sea and sky.

"Thank you for bringing me here," she said.

"Consider it your home while you are in St. Dominique, Laurel."

He drove into the graveled driveway and stopped. The front door opened and a woman hurried down the steps toward the car.

"This is Yveline," Christian said. "Yveline, this is Mademoiselle Merritt. She will be our guest for the next few weeks."

The woman smiled. "*Monsieur* has told me of your accident," she said in careful English. "Be assured that we be taking the utmost good care of you."

"Thank you," Laurel answered.

"I have prepared lunch out on the terrace, but if you prefer I could serve it in your room, *mademoiselle*."

"I'd like to be outside."

"Then we'll eat on the terrace, *s'il vous plaît*, Yveline," Christian said.

Inside the house it was pleasantly cool. The living room was large, twice the size of her mother's front parlor, and furnished in earth tones of beige and ivory, warm browns, with touches of burnt orange and lemon yellow. The white walls were hung with paintings: a small Van Gogh, a Hogarth print, and native paintings, vividly bright in movement and design. Pots of leafy green palms and ferns added color to the room. Open French doors gave a view of the sea.

"Come," Christian said, and taking Laurel's arm, led her out onto the terrace.

The sand stretched pure white down to the water. There was a dock, with a boat tied at the end.

"My one weakness," Christian said when he seated Laurel. "As soon as you're up to it we'll take a sail around the island."

"I'd like that," she said.

They ate small oysters with fresh green limes, a rich fish soup, and a heart-of-palm-and-artichoke salad. He poured white wine and said, "I asked the doctor if it was all right and he said it was. But only a little, you've had a lot of medication."

"Aye, aye, Captain." She smiled and touched her glass to his. Then her expression sobered and she said, "I haven't thanked you for being with me at the hospital, Christian. It helped to know you were there."

"That's where I wanted to be," he said. And this is where I want you to be now, he thought. Here in my home, with me.

Laurel had lost weight in the hospital. She was pale, and with her fair hair drawn back off her face she looked young and vulnerable. When, toward the end of the meal, he saw her hand tremble, he said, "Are you all right?"

She put her fork down. "I'm a little tired."

He rose, and going to her chair, he scooped her up into his arms.

"I can walk," she protested.

"But you don't have to, not as long as I'm here to carry you."

"Christian . . . ?"

He looked down at her. "Let me take care of you," he said.

For a moment Laurel hesitated, then with a sigh she rested her head against his chest. It felt solid and comforting, like the arms that held her. She would not think about why he had brought her here to his home. She only knew that she was glad he had.

He carried her down an arched corridor to a sun-filled bedroom. A bouquet of red roses stood in the middle of the dresser, gardenias floated in a crystal bowl beside the bed. French doors opened onto a private terrace.

"Yveline has unpacked for you," Christian said when he put Laurel down. "I'll call her so that she can help you undress." He opened a door to the right of her bed. "This leads to my room," he said. "I'll leave it open at night in case there's anything you need."

"I don't know what to say. I don't know how to thank you for everything you've done."

"You don't have to thank me, Laurel. All you have to do is get well."

"You're very good to me, Christian."

He touched the side of her face. "I like being good to you. I like having you in my home."

His home. Funny, that was the first time he had thought of it that way. Always before he had referred to it as his house, the place where he lived. But suddenly it had become a home. Because Laurel was here. And while he liked the feeling that it gave him, it also caused him a bit of consternation. He was a self-sufficient man, satisfied with his life exactly as it was. He would get married someday, but until he did he preferred his privacy, which was why he had never brought a woman here. Until now.

Laurel needed him. When she was better he would let her go, but for now, for this little while, he would keep her here with him.

Because he did not want to think about how it would be when she left him, Christian told her to nap and said that he would see her that night at dinner. He brushed a kiss upon her forehead. "Rest now, my dear."

She didn't want him to leave, but she summoned a smile and said, "Thank you, Christian."

Never before had she experienced the kind of tenderness Christian had shown her since the accident. Darcie Ann had been a good mother, in her way, but illness made Darcie Ann uncomfortable. Euphemia had been the one who nursed both Laurel and her sister through their childhood illnesses.

But being cared for by Christian was unlike anything she had ever experienced. He had comforted her when she'd been in pain. When she couldn't sleep he had held her hand and spoken to her in a gently soothing voice. He had helped her through a frightening and traumatic time and she would be eternally grateful to him.

But she didn't know why he had done those things. He had made it clear before the accident that he wanted no romantic entanglement, and he was so dead set against Dorset building on the chosen piece of land that obviously he didn't have a business reason for watching over her. What was it, then? She didn't understand.

Laurel slept most of the afternoon, but awakened when Yveline knocked and came into her room.

"It be after six," she said. "Monsieur Dumond said maybe you should eat dinner now."

Laurel sat up and rubbed her eyes. "Yes, I guess I should. I'll take a shower first, though."

"I be helping you."

"That's not necessary, Yveline. I can manage."

Arms crossed over her bosom, the woman regarded Laurel intently. "Monsieur Dumond told me to be watching out for you. You don't want me in there with you then I be waiting here in case you need something."

"Very well," Laurel said, feeling like she was three again and that Euphemia was glaring at her because she had done something bad.

When she came out of the shower she saw that her toiletries had been arranged, and that one of her clean nightgowns and a robe had been hung on the back of the bathroom door. Before she put them on she closed the door and looked at herself in the mirror. The cuts on her arms had almost healed, but both arms were bruised and there was an evil green bruise on one hip.

She put the gown and robe on, then brushed her hair, touched a pale coral lipstick to her lips and a dab of perfume behind her ears. That helped her feel like a woman again.

When Yveline seated her in a chaise on her terrace, she said, "I be serving dinner out here. Monsieur Dumond be right along."

Except for the soft splash of the waves against the shore it was very still. There were no boats on the horizon, only the clear blue-green water for as far as she could see. When the sun began to dip toward the sea the sky changed to a deeper blue. Patches of pink appeared and the sky caught fire and burst forth in vibrant red.

Laurel got up to stand at the railing. She wished she were an artist, wished that somehow she could capture the beauty of this moment. Leaning forward, her face enraptured, she gazed out at sea and sky.

And that was the way Christian saw her. He stood at the opening of the French doors, about to speak, but was stopped by the vision she made standing there. In the last rays of the sunset her body was clearly and beautifully outlined. He could see every gently rounded curve, the sweet contours of a ripeness of womanhood that stopped the breath in his throat.

"Laurel?"

She turned, unaware that her body was so clearly defined, that the gown had been made transparent by the sun. Christian's heart beat hard against his ribs and his body tightened with almost uncontrollable need.

"Isn't it magnificent?" she whispered, as though afraid if she spoke too loudly, she would shatter the beauty of the moment.

"Magnificent." He swallowed hard, hands clenched against his sides so that he would not reach out to her.

But it was she who held her hands out to him. "Come and see, Christian," she said. "See how beautiful it all is."

They stood together at the railing and watched while the sun disappeared into the sea. He put his arm around her waist and because Laurel could not help herself, she moved closer to him and rested her head against his shoulder. But she did not speak because it seemed to her in this moment that there was between them an almost spiritual bonding that transcended anything she had ever known before. And more, much more. For suddenly her body warmed with need. She wanted to turn to him, to kiss his mouth and feel his arms come hard around her.

With a shuddering breath, she stepped away from him. When she did he looked at her through the lowering darkness. She saw the flare of his nostrils and something in his gray eyes that she had never seen before. He seemed about to speak, but he didn't.

In the afterglow of the day, with the last rays of the sun turning the sea to gold, they ate the dinner that Yveline served. They spoke little, for there seemed no need for words. It was enough to be together like this, to listen to the waves pounding against the shore and the cry of gulls swooping low over the sea.

When it grew darker, Yveline brought candles. She cleared away the dishes and served their coffee. But still they sat, there in the candlelight, reluctant to go in.

At last Christian said, "You'd better get to bed."

"It's so lovely out here I hate to go in." Laurel tried to hold back a yawn. "But you're right, I feel as though I could sleep for a week."

She pushed her chair back, but before she could rise Christian came around the table, and as he had earlier, he picked her up in his arms. Her body was soft against his and through the silky sheerness of her gown and robe he felt the press of her breasts against his chest. Bending his head, he kissed her lightly on the lips, then turned and carried her into the bedroom and placed her on the bed.

"If you need anything during the night, just call out or ring this." He indicated a small silver bell. "I'm only a few feet away so don't hesitate. I'm a light sleeper."

Especially when you're so near, he wanted to say. Especially when I'll be able to hear your slightest movement, each whispered sigh.

Laurel looked up at him and it was all he could do not to touch her.

"Thank you," she started to say, but he put a finger against her lips.

"It means a great deal to me to know you're here, Laurel." He rested his hand against the side of her face. "Sleep well, my dear," he said.

"Good night, Christian."

She wanted him to stay here with her, the way he had at the hospital, wanted to sleep with him and awake with him. She wanted...

"Good night," she said again.

It was a long time that night before Christian slept. He lay awake, looking up at the ceiling, his whole being conscious of Laurel asleep in the next room. With every part of his being he wanted to go to her.

Oh, God, he thought. God, help me to tell her the truth. Help me not to do anything to cause her pain. Help me... He heard a muffled cry quickly smothered, and it seemed to him that he could feel her pain, that it hurt him the way it hurt her.

The accident had been his fault. He should not have sent Belain to show her the other properties, he should have taken her himself. He hadn't because being with her had become too painful for him.

He had warned Belain. "Miss Merritt is a very special business associate," he'd said. "She must be treated with the utmost respect."

Belain had put his hands on her. He had almost killed her.

Christian had gone to his room the day they released him from the hospital. "You're fired," he said. "Don't go back to the office because if you do, I'll break every bone in your body."

"The accident wasn't my fault," Belain had tried to say. "It was raining, the roads were muddy."

"I don't want any excuses, I just want you out of my sight. My secretary will send your check and collect the things from your desk." Christian had taken a step into the room. "If I ever see you anywhere near Miss Merritt again, I'll kill you. Is that clear?"

"*Je comprends.*" Belain smirked. "You want Mademoiselle Merritt for yourself, *n'est-ce pas?*"

He'd almost hit him then, hit him in spite of the abrasions on Belain's face and the bandaged ankle. It had taken every ounce of his will not to, to clench his hands to his sides and say, "Remember what I've said. Stay away from her."

Laurel murmured in her sleep. Christian waited, and when the sound came again he got up and went to stand in the open door between their rooms. She lay on her side, one hand curled near her face, her hair tumbled about the pillow. Her legs moved restlessly beneath the sheet, then she sighed and her body relaxed and her breathing evened.

He watched her for a long time, there in the silence between their two rooms. At last he turned and went back to his own bed.

And when finally he slept, her name was like a prayer upon his lips.

Chapter Six

The first morning Laurel joined Christian for breakfast on the terrace he glanced up from his newspaper in surprise.

"You're awake," he said, pleased.

"Am I disturbing you?"

"No, indeed. This is a wonderful surprise." He rose and pulled out the chair across from him. "You're sure you're up to it?"

"Absolutely." She smiled at him. "I called Eli this morning to let him know where I was."

"And?" Christian waited.

"He said to take all the time I needed."

"Three or four months?" he asked with a grin.

Maybe not that long. She looked at the half of grapefruit and coffee cup in front of him. "Is that all you eat for breakfast?"

"I'm usually in a hurry."

"Why?"

"Why?" He shrugged. "Anxious to get to the office, I suppose."

Laurel leaned back in her chair and looked out at the sea. "It's so lovely here, Christian. If I were you, I'd never want to leave. Do you ever swim before breakfast?"

"I rarely have time in the morning, but once in a while I do at night. It helps me sleep."

"Have you since I've been here?"

He looked at her over the rim of his coffee cup and shook his head. "I want to be close by in case you need me," he said.

I need you, she wanted to say. But didn't.

There had been times this past week when she had awakened in the night, conscious of him asleep in the next room. If she was very still, she could hear his breathing and she would think of how he must look lying there alone in his bed, eyes closed, his long dark lashes making patterned shadows against his face. What did he sleep in? she wondered, and pictured him in black silk pajamas. Or with nothing, his lean, dark length stretched out under the cool sheet. Alone in the stillness of the night she would feel her body warm, and know a longing she had never felt before.

And sometimes, more asleep than awake, she would feel his presence and know that he was there in the doorway of her room watching over her. Again and again she wanted to ask why he had brought her here. But she did not; it was enough to be with him.

After that first morning Christian began to look forward to having breakfast with Laurel. Instead of his usual half grapefruit and coffee, scarcely tasted while he perused the morning paper, he began to have what Yveline called "real food."

With a wide smile she served them papaya and bananas, mangoes and guavas, omelets filled with melted cheese and mushrooms, or strawberry waffles with thick maple syrup.

"I'm going to gain five pounds a day if this keeps up," Christian complained. But he would gladly have gained any amount if it meant having breakfast with Laurel every morning. She had put back a little of the weight she had lost in the hospital, and now with the bit of a tan she'd acquired she looked very beautiful, and infinitely desirable. But that was something Christian didn't want to think about.

Every evening before supper they walked on the beach, not very far at first, but farther as Laurel's strength returned. On the weekend of the second week she was there she told him she would like to go swimming.

"All right," he said, "but only when I'm with you so I can keep an eye on you."

He kept an eye on her, all right. In fact he couldn't take his eyes off her. When she came out of the house in a white bikini he thought, *Mon Dieu!* and it was all he could do to keep his hands off her. She was perfection from the top of the blond hair that she'd pinned up on her head down to her pink-polished toenails. Her breasts were full and gently rounded, her waist was small, and the bottom half of the bikini covered her like a second skin.

His body tightened, he felt himself grow. "Ready?" he managed to croak, and turning away, he started into the water and didn't stop until he was waist high. Dammit, he was thirty-six years old, not some teenager with raging hormones who could get an erection by just looking at a girl. But Laurel was not a girl, she was a woman. The most exciting woman he had ever known. And God help him, he wanted her as he had never wanted a woman before.

Cursing under his breath, Christian dived through a wave, swam hard, and when he surfaced, panting for air, some of the tension had eased.

They swam side by side for a little while. The sky was a clear clean blue, the water a sparkling turquoise. "Don't tire yourself," he warned her.

"I won't." She sighed. "This is wonderful, Christian. You're so lucky to live here." She rolled onto her back and looked up at the sky, her body relaxed, letting the waves cradle and rock her. Her eyes were closed, her face was toward the sun. Droplets of water glistened on her suntanned skin, and a slight smile played across her mouth. She seemed a part of the sea and the sky as she floated motionless on the gentle crest of the waves.

They were where they could touch bottom now, and instead of swimming, Christian walked beside her, so intent in watching her that he did not see the wave that was bigger than the other waves until it lifted her high away from him. He reached out for her, their bodies brushed, then the wave covered her. She came up sputtering and he grabbed her and put his arms around her waist.

She laughed and rested her hands on his shoulders. "I didn't see it coming. I . . ." Another wave brought them closer. The laughter died.

She whispered his name, "Christian," and he kissed her.

A saltwater kiss, wet and warm and wonderful.

They clung to each other, letting the waves carry them closer to shore, her arms around his neck, his hands on her waist, mouth against mouth, tongues seeking and tasting. He felt his body grow rigid as it had when he had seen her earlier, but now he wasn't ashamed, because there was a fever in him that he could no longer control.

He brought her closer. They kissed again. She felt his hardness but she didn't move away. He spread his legs and when he cupped her bottom and brought her tight against him, she moaned deep in her throat.

The sound of her desire set the blood pounding in his veins. He wanted to take her here, wanted to strip their suits away and join his body to hers.

He rained kisses over her face, down her throat, nuzzling, nipping. He shoved the bikini top down and took her salt-slick breasts in his hands, lifting them, burying his face against them. He tasted salt, and her.

She leaned into him, hips thrust forward, and cradled his head between her hands. "Christian," she whispered. "Oh, Christian."

"Laurel!" Her name was a hoarse and primitive cry there in the silence of the sea because he knew now that she wanted him as much as he wanted her, knew that he could make love with her here. And afterward he would lay her upon his bed and . . .

No! Oh, God, no! He couldn't. Not until she knew. But if she knows, a voice inside his head said, it will be finished between us. Take her now while you can. Take her here. . . .

He held her away from him. The sunlight was on her face. Her lips were parted, her eyes were slumberous, drugged with desire.

He put his hands on her shoulders. "You're... you're not strong yet. You need more time. You..."

Tell her! the voice inside his head cried.

But he shook his head, denying it, and tightening his hands on her shoulders, said, "I'm sorry." Then, before she could speak, he turned away from her and headed, as though the devil himself were after him, toward the shore.

Laurel stood ankle deep in the water, her back toward the house so she would not see Christian. One moment her body had been tingling and alive, crying out with the need to be joined to Christian. The next moment she had been alone.

Never again, she promised herself. Never again would she allow him to do what he had just done, then leave her shaking with need. He had said she wasn't strong enough, that she needed more time, but she knew that wasn't the reason.

Tomorrow she would leave his house and his island. She would go away, and God help her, maybe in time she would be able to forget him.

At last she turned toward the house. He was gone, but she saw Yveline coming toward her with a robe.

"You best be going in to shower," the black woman said as she placed the terry-cloth robe around Laurel's shoulders. "Monsieur Dumond say that when you are ready he will see you on the patio."

"Please tell Monsieur Dumond that I'm a little tired," Laurel said. "I'd like to bathe and then rest.

And if it's not too much trouble, Yveline, I'd appreciate it if I could have dinner in my room tonight."

"Of course, *mademoiselle*. It is nothing of trouble. I will tell *monsieur* and I am sure he will understand. I will bring you a nice cup of tea, yes? It will restore the color to your cheeks and then you will rest."

Laurel put her hand on the other woman's arm. "Thank you," she said, feeling the sudden sting of tears behind her eyelids. "Yes, I would like a cup of tea."

When she went into her room she closed her door, and the connecting door between her and Christian's rooms. She would have her dinner here tonight, and stay in her room until he left in the morning. Then she would leave.

She took a hot and stinging shower, letting the water beat hard over her head and down her body, trying to wash away the memory of his touch and of the fire that had kindled and grown within her.

"Never again," she said aloud, pounding the wall with wet fists while her tears mingled with the cascade of water. "Never again!"

When she came out of the shower and dressed in a nightgown and robe, she did not go out onto the terrace. In a little while Yveline came in with a dinner tray. Laurel tried to eat, but could do little more than pick at the crabmeat cocktail before she put the tray aside and began to pack.

And finally, when it was very late, she turned off the light inside her room and opened the doors leading out to her balcony.

She sat in a deck chair and watched the half-moon rise. A million stars came out and the air smelled of the sea. It was as beautiful a night as she had ever seen, so beautiful it made her throat ache with unshed tears. The sand stretched pale in the moonlight, white-capped waves rolled into shore. Far in the distance she could see the lights of a cruise ship.

The hour grew late. At last she stood, about to go in, then turned once more to look out at the sea and sky. And saw Christian coming up out of the water.

He came up onto the beach and stood there, naked in the moonlight, sluicing water off his body, running his hands through his short curly hair. And when he had done that he stood, legs apart, looking toward the house.

Laurel shrank back into the shadows. He couldn't see her but she could see him. His body was perfectly outlined against the moon, strong and pure of form, magnificently masculine.

She put her fist against her mouth so that she wouldn't cry out, and there in the moonlight she memorized every perfect line of his body.

He started toward the house and when he drew nearer he stopped and looked toward her room. He stood there for several minutes, then he started forward, and stopped. It seemed to her as though she could see his shoulders sag. Then they straightened and he turned and went up the back steps and into the house.

But Laurel stayed where she was for a little while longer. Until finally, exhausted by the day and by the emotions churning inside her, she went back into her room.

. . . Hush little baby, don't you cry . . .

"It's raining, Daddy. I don't like the rain. It scares me. Daddy? Daddy?"

He didn't answer. She called again and again, but there was only silence, and the rain.

She was in a car. The road was narrow. She looked down and saw that the road dropped away to sheer nothingness. She tightened her hands on the wheel. Her whole body was tight, so tight her skin hurt. She knew that something bad was going to happen.

The rain slashed against the window. She couldn't see and she began to moan, peering through the rain and the darkness, scrubbing at the clouded windshield.

The beam of the headlights came around the side of the mountain straight toward her. She cried out. The lights came nearer. She pounded her fist against the horn, but no sound came. She looked at the drop on one side, the sheer rock face of the mountain on the other.

"No!" she cried. "No!"

Crush of metal, breaking glass. She screamed.

"Laurel!"

She couldn't stop screaming.

"Laurel, wake up!"

She clung to him, still gripped by the terror of the nightmare.

"Shh," he whispered. "It's all right, *ma petite.* I'm with you, Laurel. You're safe, my dear. Safe here with me."

Christian laid her down but she would not let go of him, and so he lay beside her and gathered her in his arms.

"I'm here with you, Laurel," he said again and again. "You're safe, *ma chère*. I won't let anything happen to you."

She buried her face against his shoulder, her throat catching with gulps of receding fear, shudders trembling through her body.

Christian held her close, one hand against the back of her head. He stroked her hair. He spoke softly, reassuringly.

She heard the rain more clearly now. "Don't leave me," she said, afraid the dream would come again.

"I won't." He kissed the top of her head. "Go to sleep, Laurel. I'm right here with you now."

Her body was warm against his. He could feel every line, every contour. With every trembling movement he felt the press of her breasts against his bare chest. He breathed in the scent of her skin, and felt the wetness of tears against his throat. He knew desire, and quelled it. He held her as gently as he would hold a child, and soothed her until at last she became quiet and he knew that she slept.

And still he held her, and whispered words in French that even if she were awake she would not understand. He did not sleep, but lay staring at the ceiling, warmed by her body so close to his. This is what it would be like to sleep with her every night, he thought. This is what it would be like to breathe in her scent and feel her softness next to me.

He listened to the waves breaking against the shore. He heard the cry of a gull and the whisper of wind through the palms. He felt her breath against his skin.

He murmured her name into the silence of the room, and knew that tomorrow he would have to tell her.

He was gone when Laurel awoke the next morning. But the pillow next to hers still showed where his head had lain. She rested her hand there, and when she closed her eyes she could see him as he had been coming from the sea, naked and splendid in the moonlight.

She remembered the terror of her nightmare. She must have cried out and Christian had come to her. He had held her with gentleness and she had gone to sleep in his arms.

She lay for a long time, thinking, wondering. He was probably the kindest man she had ever known. And gentle. He was also a sexual man, and that was what puzzled her. His desire for her was real, yet each time they had come close to making love he had pulled away from her. She did not know why. Before she left him she had to know.

When Yveline came in with a breakfast tray, Laurel asked, "Has *monsieur* left for his office yet?"

"No, *mademoiselle*. He is waiting to see you. I am to let him know when you have finished breakfast."

Laurel took a deep breath. "Tell him . . ." She wet her lips. "Tell him in half an hour, Yveline. And thank you for bringing my breakfast."

"Monsieur told me to. He said that very likely you were tired and needed to rest this morning."

When Yveline left, Laurel drank her coffee and ate part of a piece of toast. Nothing else. Her stomach was in knots, she was too nervous to eat.

She put on a pink flowered sundress, got her suitcase ready and went out onto her balcony, and that's where she was when Christian knocked and came in.

His face was drawn. There were shadows of fatigue under his gray eyes. "How do you feel?" he asked.

"I'm fine, Christian. Thank you for coming in last night."

He nodded. "I heard you cry out in your sleep. It was the accident, wasn't it? You heard the rain. I suppose that triggered the nightmare."

"Yes, probably. I'm sorry—"

"Please." He stopped her. "Please don't apologize because you had a nightmare. I . . ." He saw the suitcase on the bed. His face tightened and he said, "Are you planning to leave?"

"Yes." Laurel hesitated. "It's time I did, Christian."

"I see." He took a steadying breath. "I won't try to keep you here if you're determined to leave, but first I'd like you to take a drive with me."

"A drive?" She looked puzzled. "Where?"

"Up into the mountains. I'd like you to meet my grandmother and my sister."

"Your grandmother?"

"My sister lives with her, she and her little boy."

"The boy that broke his arm?"

"Etienne. Yes."

"I'd planned on leaving this morning."

"Another day won't matter.'

She didn't understand. Why he would want her to meet his grandmother and sister?

"You can leave tomorrow," he said.

Laurel took a deep breath. "Is what I'm wearing all right?"

"Yes, but take a sweater. It gets cool in the mountains later in the day." A muscle jumped in his cheek. "I'll wait for you in the car."

Laurel stood in the middle of the room, staring at the door after he had closed it. She had no idea why he wanted her to meet his family, or why she had agreed to stay this extra day.

But she would because it meant another day with Christian. And because she had to know what it was that was keeping them apart.

Chapter Seven

They left the house right after breakfast. Christian had little to say. He simply told her they were going to the village of Le Carbet, and that it was a two-hour drive.

His expression was grim, his jaw tight. He stared straight ahead, but drove carefully so as not to alarm her on the curves as they climbed higher into the mountains.

Time and again Laurel looked at him, almost unmindful of the beauty of the scenery, concerned by the obvious strain Christian was under, filled with a sense of foreboding she could not give name to.

After almost an hour of silence, she said, "Tell me about your grandmother and your sister. And your parents. Are they alive?"

He shook his head. "My mother and father were killed in a boating accident when I was six and Solange was four. My grandmother raised us." He manipulated a dangerous curve before he went on. "When my grandfather died *Grandmère* took over running the sugarcane plantation. She's in her late seventies now and still running things, up at dawn and out in the field supervising the workers, checking on everything." The shadow of a smile relaxed his face for a moment. "We have an overseer who's been with us for years, but *Grandmère* is the boss. Solange keeps the books and manages the household."

"Are you and your sister close?"

Christian nodded. "Even as children we rarely had the usual brother-and-sister squabbles, perhaps because we were so young when our parents died. I've always been protective of Solange. Her husband died two years ago and she and Etienne have lived with my grandmother since then." He glanced at Laurel. "I want you to meet my family," he said.

Why? she wondered. Why now? Christian had never, even in the slightest way, indicated that what was between them was serious. Why then, on her last day, was he taking her to meet his family?

The road wound farther up into the mountains. The air was cooler here, the vegetation even fuller and lusher. Bamboo, thatch palms, palmettos and ferns lined both sides of the narrow road. Wild orchids grew among the sheltering greenery.

They came around a curve and ahead of her Laurel saw a village. "Le Carbet," Christian said.

There was a white church that looked like the country churches in Georgia, a school, a grocery store, a fruit market, and a few one-story office buildings that faced a palm-lined central plaza. There were people on the street and children playing in the plaza.

"The plantation's only a few miles from the village," Christian said, and his hands tightened so hard on the steering wheel that his knuckles looked stark white against the tan of his skin.

A mile out of town they came to the fields of sugar-cane that stretched for as far as Laurel could see. "This is our land." Christian gestured with a wide sweep of his arm. "We have almost ten thousand acres." He slowed the car and almost reluctantly said, "There's the house, there through the trees."

It looked not unlike the antebellum homes Laurel had seen in Louisiana and Mississippi, not too unlike her home, but larger, clean white against the blue St. Dominican sky, surrounded by palms and cypress hung with silvery Spanish moss.

He turned into a sand-pebbled driveway and stopped in front of the house. "This is *Le Château Dumond,*" he said. But he did not look at her.

The front door opened. An elderly, quite handsome black woman came out. She stood poised for a moment, then with a glad cry she came down the steps and hurried toward the car, crying, "*Mon très cher petit fils.* Why did you not tell me you were coming?"

"*Comme c'est bon d'être ici avec toi, Grandmère.* How good it is to be here with you, Grandmother." Christian got out of the car to meet her. She enfolded him into her arms, kissed both his cheeks and held him away from her. "You are tired, *non?* I think you have been working too hard." She smiled at Laurel. "Forgive me," she said, "I'm so delighted to see my grandson that I have forgotten my manners. I am Marie Dumond."

Dumond? Laurel looked from the black woman to Christian.

"Laurel . . ." He took a deep breath, and with his arm still around Marie Dumond he said, "Laurel, this is my grandmother. Grandmother, this is Laurel Merritt."

Automatic good manners helped Laurel to get out of the car and offer her hand. *"Madame,"* she said.

His grandmother?

But Marie Dumond was black.

"You are visiting in St. Dominique, *mademoiselle?"*

"Yes." Laurel took a steadying breath. She did not look at Christian. "I came here on business but I've stayed longer than I intended to."

"Laurel was in an accident two weeks ago, *Grandmère,"* Christian said in a voice that did not sound like his voice. "She's been staying at the house so Yveline could look after her."

"Très bien, Christian. It would have been very bad to let her stay alone in a hotel, *non?"* She looked at Laurel, her expression kind and concerned. "But you have recovered?"

"Yes, thank you."

Laurel truly did not know what to say or do. She was in a state of shock, all sorts of thoughts and emotions scrambling through her brain. Why hadn't Christian told her that he was black? He didn't look black, he looked . . . tanned.

"I love your tan," Virgie had said.

All right, Laurel told herself. It's possible even though he doesn't look black. He's French, too. This is the Caribbean. The mixture of races has been going on here for almost four hundred years. You see it on all of the islands: dark-skinned people with blue eyes, light-skinned people with negroid features. But Christian . . . ?

Why hadn't he told her?

Like an automaton Laurel let his grandmother lead her into the house. Christian followed a few paces behind. He didn't speak, he didn't take her arm.

Inside the house it was pleasantly cool. There were beautifully tiled floors in the living room, French provincial furniture, antiques. Marie Dumond led them into a patiolike room. White wicker furniture here, colorful cushions, greenery.

"Would you like tea, Mademoiselle Merritt? Or perhaps something stronger? I myself like a drink before lunch. Our cook makes a splendid planter's punch. Will you join me in one?"

Yes, a drink. My God, a drink. "Thank you, *madame*," Laurel said.

"Marie," the grandmother said. "*S'il vous plaît*, call me Marie." She smiled at Christian. "And you, *mon cher?*"

"The same," he said.

"*Bon.* If you will excuse me for a moment, I will go and tell cook that we will be five for lunch. Solange went to pick up Etienne but she will be back soon."

They were alone.

"Your grandmother is very nice," Laurel said.

"Yes." He leaned forward in his chair, hands clasped between his knees. "I should have told you," he said.

"Yes, you should have."

"I wanted to, but I—"

"Uncle Christian!" A small boy ran into the room. "I didn't know you were coming. Mama didn't tell me. How long are you going to stay? Can we go fishing tomorrow?"

Christian stood and scooped the boy up, careful of the left arm that was in a cast. "Slow down, Etienne," he said. "I'd like you to meet someone." He put the boy down. "Etienne, this is Miss Merritt from the United States. Laurel, this is my nephew, Etienne.'

His skin was chocolate brown, his eyes a sparkling black. He had the longest eyelashes Laurel had ever seen, and when he smiled she saw that two of his front teeth were missing.

"How do you do?" she said.

"Bonjour, mademoiselle."

"I heard you broke your arm."

"I fell out of a tree," he said. "It hurt a lot but I didn't cry...." He shrugged thin shoulders. "At least, not very much. Uncle Christian came and took me to the doctor in Port-au-Mer and the doctor said I was the best..." He looked at Christian.

"Patient," Christian said.

"Yes. That I was the best patient he'd ever had." He came across the room and, holding his arm out to Laurel, said, "Would you like to write something on my cast?"

"Yes, of course." She opened her purse and looked for a pen.

"Here," Christian said, offering one from his jacket pocket.

She took it. They didn't look at each other. She drew a picture of a palm tree and of a small figure halfway between the palm fronds and the earth, a stick figure, arms and legs akimbo.

Etienne, intrigued, came to lean close to her. "That's me!" he exclaimed.

"Christian?" a voice said from the doorway. "I didn't know you were coming today."

"Come look, Mama." Etienne held his arm out. "See what the lady drew on my cast."

Christian's sister came into the room. Almost as tall as Christian, she was one of the most beautiful women Laurel had ever seen. Perfect skin, of a light cinnamon color, green oval-shaped eyes, a straight nose, a full mouth. Her hair, as black and curly as Christian's, was pulled straight off her face into a classic chignon. Gold looped earrings hung from her ears, and like Laurel, she too wore a sundress.

Christian went to embrace her. She kissed both his cheeks, as her grandmother had done then, stepping away from him, smiled at Laurel.

"This is Laurel Merritt, Solange Villefort," Christian said.

Solange crossed the room and, offering her hand to Laurel, said, "I'm happy to meet you, Miss Merritt." And though her smile was friendly, her green eyes questioned.

Laurel stared at her. Something...a memory she couldn't quite capture startled her. Solange reminded her of someone she'd met a long time ago. Someone...

"How do you do," she said.

Christian's grandmother came in, followed by a servant with a tray of drinks and hors d'oeuvres. Laurel sipped the planter's punch. She spoke when she was spoken to. She asked Etienne about his school. She answered Marie Dumond's questions about her family.... "Yes, *madame,* we're from the South. I work for a large hotel chain. Public relations. Yes, I like what I do."

And every time she looked at Solange she tried to remember who it was Solange reminded her of.

But it was not until they were having lunch that it came back to her, a childhood memory of a woman she had met only once.

Velma Johnson. Yes, that was her name, and she had been, like Solange, a handsome black woman.

There was one more week left before summer vacation. She was in the fifth grade and she had stopped in at her father's office at the newspaper to tell him about the end-of-the-term picnic. There had been a woman in the office with him, a black woman. Her father had said, "Laurel honey, this is Miss Velma Johnson. She's from Detroit."

She remembered the woman's smile, she remembered how pretty she had been. But she hadn't offered her hand because her mother had told her you don't shake hands with Negroes.

It had been in the sixties, during the freedom marches. Years later she learned that her father had written an editorial against segregation that had brought the wrath of the town down upon his head, and Velma Johnson into his office to thank him.

The incident of meeting the colored lady had stayed with Laurel for a few days, but so much happened that summer that she'd forgotten all about her. There'd been the civil rights marches, pictures in the newspapers and on television of police with clubs and fire hoses. People had been beaten and thrown in jail. Protesters, both black and white, had died. A black minister by the name of Martin Luther King emerged as a leader of his people.

And her father died.

Her auntie Maudie May took her to the hospital. "So you can tell your daddy goodbye," her aunt said. And when they reached the hospital Maudie May's husband, Willard, said, "You be a brave little girl now, hear?" And just as he took her hand to lead her down the hall to her father's room, she had seen the woman she had met in her father's office standing all alone near the stairs.

Her father had died that night. Two months later Laurel learned of the "Merritt family scandal."

Reading had been her one refuge from the grief that followed her father's death. Only in books could she escape from the sad and terrible fact that she would never see him again. On the day it happened she had gone into the library, the room her father had loved the most. She had settled herself in his big office chair, turned away from his desk to catch the afternoon sun, and she had been reading *archy and mehitabel*.

She'd stopped at the word transmigrated, pondering on it when the door to the library opened and her aunt Emily Rose and Miss Lucinda Udell came in.

"It was a terrible thing," Aunt Emily Rose said in a hushed voice. "Just terrible. Phillip was actually going to leave Darcie Ann for that...that woman."

"I declare," Miss Udell said.

"Velma Johnson. A negra! All I can say is thank the good Lord he had the grace to die before it happened."

Then her mother's voice had called out, "Emily Rose? Lucinda? Lunch is ready."

Laurel had stared down at the page, only the words swam before her eyes. Daddy, she had thought. Daddy.

She had buried the memory of that afternoon deep inside her. She had never spoken of it to her mother, had never told that she knew about the black woman her father had almost left them for. She had not thought of it for years. Not until today.

Laurel looked across the table at Solange Dumond. Had it been true? she wondered. Had her father loved the woman named Velma Johnson?

Other thoughts... What would her mother think if she found out that Christian was part black? What would Virgie say? What would their friends think?

The conversation turned to the reason she had come to St. Dominique, and to her accident.

"Jean-Louis Belain? That dreadful man!" Solange said when she learned that he had been driving the day of the accident. "*Mon Dieu,* Christian, why did you send Mademoiselle Merritt out with him?"

"It was a mistake." Christian looked at Laurel, then away. "I shouldn't have."

Nor should he have brought her here. He knew that now. He had seen the shock in her eyes when she realized Marie was his grandmother, that little Etienne was his nephew. She had tried to be pleasant but she had barely spoken all through lunch.

He should have told her the night they'd met in Atlanta. He should have said, "I'm black. Regardless of the color of my skin, or that I am also of French and Indian blood, I am black."

But he hadn't because she was Southern. Because he'd had experience with her kind of woman before. He had known how she would react if he told her.

And because he had felt something when they'd kissed that he had never felt before, he had left Atlanta. To avoid a problem, he had told himself. To stop whatever it was that might be between them before it started.

He'd known it would make a difference to her. It had happened before, not as often as it used to, but there were still those occasional times when someone asked, "Your background is French?" and he had answered, "French, Carib Indian, and African," because he was proud of who he was, proud of his heritage, of the mixture of blood that ran through his veins. But in spite of his pride, he had never quite gotten used to that subtle change of expression when he said the word African.

When Laurel had come to St. Dominique he had dared to hope that it might be different with her. From their very first meeting the attraction between them had been strong. He had felt for her an emotion he had never felt for a woman before. He had known he should tell her the truth about his race, but he hadn't. Instead he had drawn away from her. He'd asked

Jean-Louis to drive her around the island, and because he had, she had almost been killed.

Last night when he had held her in his arms he had known he had to tell her the truth. That was why he had brought her here to Le Carbet to meet his family. He had seen the shock in her eyes when he introduced his grandmother, he had heard it in her voice. He knew that she was no different than the others.

As soon after lunch as he could he said, "It's time Laurel and I started back to Port-au-Mer."

Etienne, lower lip stuck out in a pout, said, "But I want you to stay, Uncle Christian. I want Miss Laurel to draw some more pictures for me."

"Next time, Etienne," Christian said, knowing there would be no next time.

He wanted to get this over with, yet he dreaded the thought of being alone with Laurel. He didn't want to face her anger or her scorn. Tomorrow she would leave, and though he had known it was inevitable, especially now that she had learned the truth, the thought of losing her was like a visceral pain that tore at his insides.

His grandmother and Solange walked them to the car. Etienne held on to Laurel's hand.

"Come back soon so you can draw me some more pictures," the boy said.

Laurel brushed her hand across the top of his curly hair. But she did not answer.

While his grandmother embraced Christian, Solange said to Laurel, "It's been a pleasure meeting you, Laurel. I hope you'll return soon."

"I'll very likely be going back to the States in a day or two," Laurel said. "But thank you, Solange."

"Christian has never brought a woman friend here before. I rather hoped..." She shrugged her elegant shoulders and with a smile said, "I like you, Laurel. Please come back to us whenever you can."

Christian opened the door on her side of the car. She offered her hand to his grandmother, and was surprised when Marie Dumond put her arms around her and kissed her cheek. "It has been a pleasure to meet you, *ma chère,*" the older woman said. "I hope that Christian will bring you back to us soon."

Laurel forced a smile. "I loved being here," she answered.

"We really must be going if we're going to reach the city by dark," Christian cut in.

"Goodbye, *madame.*" Laurel squeezed the other woman's hand. "Goodbye, Etienne. Take good care of your arm."

"Come back soon," he said.

Then they were in the car, driving away from the house. Laurel looked back at the three of them standing together on the slope of lawn: his grandmother, his nephew, his sister. She waved and they waved back before the car rounded a bend in the road and they were lost from view.

They didn't speak. When they neared the city he asked if she was hungry.

"No," she said.

After that there was no conversation until they reached his home. He stopped the car and hands on the steering wheel, he said, "You're planning to leave tomorrow?"

"I don't know."

He looked at her. "But I thought—"

"You thought wrong." She got out of the car and slammed the door.

Christian stared after her, too surprised to answer. When he went into the house he saw her standing out on the balcony off the living room. She looked out at the sea, her back to him. His muscles tightened, but this had to be faced.

He went to her. "I know how you feel," he said. "I know—"

Laurel turned on him, her eyes snapping with anger. "You *don't* know," she said. "You don't know anything about me. Not one damn thing!"

"Laurel..." He took a deep breath, bracing himself. "Listen," he said. "You know now. Okay? There's no need to discuss it. You'll leave and whatever there was between us will be finished."

He started to turn away but she grabbed his arm, stopping him, her expression so angry he thought for a moment she was going to strike him. "Don't you dare walk away from me again," she said. "Don't you dare!"

"Laurel, listen—"

"No, you listen. We've both known from almost the moment we met that there was something between us. Yet you've deliberately pushed me away from you because you didn't trust me enough to tell me the truth. You just assumed that your having mixed blood would make a difference."

"Doesn't it?"

She hesitated. "I don't know," she said, and some of the anger went out of her voice. "I only know that when I'm with you I feel a sense of rightness that I've never felt before. Never, anywhere, with anyone."

She looked up at him. "That's why you've pushed me away, isn't it, Christian? You thought that if I knew, it would end between us. That I would turn and walk away from you."

"You're a Southern woman." His voice was so taut, his throat so tightly constricted he could barely speak. "I know how you feel about people like me. I've met your family. I know how they feel."

"I'm not my family. And you don't know how I feel." She shook her head. "How could you when I don't know myself?"

He felt as though he were drowning. "It could never work," he said. "We could never—"

"Don't . . . don't say anything." Laurel leaned her head against his shoulder. "Just hold me."

He put his arms around her and she felt the frantic beating of his heart against her breast. This is so hard for him, she thought. It's up to me now, I have to make this easier for him.

"I'm not going to leave tomorrow," she said.

"Are you sure?" It was difficult for him to speak.

"I'm sure," she said.

They stood without speaking, their arms around each other, and watched the sun, like a big ball of fire, sink slowly into the blue-green waters of the Caribbean.

In a little while Yveline served their dinner and they ate, there on the patio in the gathering darkness. They spoke little, but again and again their eyes met across the candlelit table.

When the hour grew late Christian took her hand and they went into the house.

Chapter Eight

Christian hesitated at the door of her room. "Come in," she said.

"Are you sure?"

"I've been sure since that first night in Atlanta."

"We're different. Your family—"

She put a finger against his lips, silencing him. "I told you," she said. "I'm not my family. I'm me, Laurel, and I know what I'm doing."

"Do you? Do you understand that once we cross this particular threshold there might not be any turning back?"

Laurel began to unbutton his shirt. "I understand." She rested the palm of her hand against his skin and felt the sharp intake of his breath. "It's all right, Christian," she said softly. "It's going to be all right."

He wanted her with a desire that bordered on madness, yet he held himself back, afraid to let go, afraid to trust the emotion welling inside him. In his heart he knew that what he felt for Laurel was not a casual thing. If they stepped across the barrier he had tried to erect between them, there would be no going back, and it would end, as surely it must, with pain.

He gripped her shoulders. "I've wanted you since that night in the hotel garden in Atlanta," he said. "My body hurt with wanting you. That's why I left, Laurel, because I knew if I stayed, it would have happened." He tightened his hands on her shoulders. "I didn't want you to come to St. Dominique. But you came."

"Yes." Her eyes met his, proud, unashamed.

A sigh shuddered through him. "I've never wanted a woman the way I want you."

She leaned her body close to his. She felt his tension, the barely restrained power within him, and while there was a part of her that was afraid of the future, there was an excitement in the fear and, like him, a desire too long held in check.

Stepping away from him, she reached around to unzip the sundress. She let it fall and stepped out of it.

Clad only in a white silk-and-lace bra, white silk bikini panties and high-heeled white sandals, with her golden hair streaming about her shoulders, she was so beautiful she took his breath. A muscle in his jaw quivered. *"Mon Dieu,"* he whispered. *"Mon Dieu."*

He unfastened the bra and cupped her breasts. He kissed her as he held her there and his mouth was warm and hungry. It seemed to Laurel as though she were slipping away from reality, melting into him as a liquid fire spread through her veins.

He took her mouth. She felt the touch of his tongue against hers. He ran his thumbs across breasts that ached for his touch. He slipped the white satin panties down over her hips and held her away from him. His breath was coming fast, his eyes were hooded, his nostrils flared with a passion too long held in check. He ran his hands over her shoulders, over her breasts, her hips.

He reached for her but she said, "Wait. Let me undress you." She unfastened the buckle of his belt. She pulled his shirt up, unbuttoned it, took it off his shoulders and tossed it aside. With unsteady hands she unzipped his trousers.

It was hard to breathe, harder to stand there and let her do this to him. He kicked his shoes off and yanked at his socks. She pulled the trousers down over his hips. Now he wore only tight black briefs.

"Take them off," she whispered.

He looked at her. "You do it," he said.

Her hands felt hot on his skin, so hot he flinched. But he made himself wait while she slipped the briefs down over his hips.

He heard the intake of her breath. He saw in her the same desire that burned like a raging fire in him.

She looked at him standing naked before her. The first time she had seen him she had sensed an animal magnetism, a hint of something primeval. She knew now that what she had only imagined was true. He was magnificent, man at his finest, powerful and beautiful.

Christian brought her back into his arms. They kissed and he said, "I can't wait any longer."

"Nor can I."

He picked her up and carried her to the bed. He laid her down, then bent to take her sandals off. She shivered and he came up beside her.

"I wanted to go slowly the first time," he said. "I wanted to relish every moment, to touch you and kiss you. But I can't, Laurel. I can't."

He covered her with his body. He took her mouth, and with a low moan of need he joined his body to hers.

She cried out, involuntarily cried with the joy of having him inside her. Her body rose to meet his, welcoming him, holding him, rejoicing in him.

He thrust deep and hard. He withdrew and thrust again and again. "So good," he murmured against her mouth. "So good, my Laurel."

His Laurel. Oh, yes. His in this intensity of a feeling unlike any other. His in total surrender. Her hands tightened on his shoulders. She turned her head and licked his skin. She put one hand, palm flat, against the small of his back to urge him on, glorying in the miracle of their two bodies that had become one, loving what he was doing to her, loving...

She tried to hold back but she couldn't. Her body rose to his and he moved hard against her. "Oh, please..." The words became incoherent, smothered against his shoulder. "Please, please, please, please..."

He cupped her head with one hand, fingers splayed against her scalp, turning her face to his. His mouth covered her mouth. "Give me your cry," he demanded. "Give it to me, Laurel."

His body thundered against hers, hard, unrelenting. And she cried her cry into his mouth as his body exploded over hers.

She had never known such an intensity of feeling, had not known what it meant to lose control of her body, to plead for release, to be so completely a part of another human being.

He rained kisses over her face. He stroked her hair. He told her how beautiful she was, how fine. He held her and soothed her. He said, *"Ma très chère. Ma chérie. Mon amour."* Words she did not quite understand, words she loved to hear.

He put his arms around her and held her close. He didn't know what tomorrow would bring, he wasn't sure that what they had done was right. But he would never be sorry it had happened. Never before, never with anyone, had he felt what he had just experienced with Laurel. When her warmth had closed about him he had known he was as near to heaven as he would ever be. She was everything he had ever dreamed of in a woman. She was fire and warmth, tenderness and passion. She was everything, for whatever time they shared, for however long it could last.

Laurel awakened as the first light of dawn streaked the sky, and when she opened her eyes she saw Christian beside her, watching her.

"Bonjour, ma petite amour," he said. "Did you sleep well?"

"Yes," Laurel said. "Oh, yes."

He saw the warmth of her smile, the sunshine in her eyes, and relief flooded through him, for he had been afraid that she would have regrets, that in the cool, clear light of day she would think of what they had done and be sorry. But there was no sorrow in her eyes; there was only happiness.

He brought her closer and held her in his arms without speaking, filled with a contentment he had never felt before.

She stroked his shoulders and his back, and when he nuzzled his face against her throat she kissed the top of his head. And knew that what she was feeling now was very right and very good.

Making love with Christian had been inevitable; she had known that almost from the time she had first seen him, and known somehow, deep in her bones, that one day they would be like this.

He raised himself on one elbow and looked down at her. He smoothed her tangled hair back from her face and kissed her lips. *"Ma très chère,"* he said. "My lovely Laurel."

He got up and, going to the windows that faced the sea, he opened the drapes. Sunlight flooded the room. "I want to see you this way," he said when he came back to her and lowered the sheet. "I want to see the sun shining on your body."

With the light at his back he was indistinct, a dark form there in the silence of the room. But, oh, such a perfect form. A beautifully sculptured head, the long slender neck that tapered down to a broadness of shoulder, the wide and muscled chest, the narrowness of waist and hip and long, straight legs. He moved toward her. She saw the ripple of his muscles, saw him grow hard with desire. Because of me, she thought. Because of me.

She whispered his name, "Christian." She felt the beat of her heart against her ribs and her body grow warm with need.

He stood above her for a moment, then he came in beside her and drew her into his arms. His mouth found hers and he kissed her with a hunger and a passion that left her breathless. When he freed her mouth he began to kiss her eyelids, her nose, her cheeks, and when she turned her head toward his throat she felt the frantic beat of his pulse against her lips.

He trailed a line of kisses down her throat, to her shoulders, her breasts. He stroked them so gently, then took a peaked nipple into his mouth.

She sighed with pleasure. Threading her fingers through his hair, she said, "Yes, oh, yes, that's nice."

He teased with his tongue, and his fingers stroked her other breast until, no longer able to bear it, she said, "No more. Oh, Christian. Please. Oh, darling, please."

Darling. The word a shimmering symphony on her lips.

He came up over her. He kissed her mouth. "Now?" he asked.

"Yes," she said. "Oh, yes."

He grasped her hips. "Laurel," he cried and joined his body to hers.

He moved against her slowly, deeply. She lifted her body to his, holding him as he held her. And dug her fingers into his shoulders to urge him on.

He began to move wildly and unrestrainedly against her. He held her with his hands, gripped her with his legs.

And she loved it. Loved him.

The breath came hard in his throat. "Now!" he whispered in an agonized voice. "Now!"

It was as it had been. Better. Unbelievable. He took her to heights she had never reached before, to a plane of ecstasy she would never have believed possible. She clung to him, heart beating against his heart, whispering his name again and again until at last she fell back into the safety of his arms.

He stroked her love-damp body, he kissed her trembling lips. Like a litany of prayer he said her name over and over again. His body felt cleansed, renewed, surfeited. He had never felt so good, so totally relaxed. It was as though his bones had melted. Yes, melted and merged with her bones, with her body. And he knew that whatever might happen now he would never be sorry that this magic had passed between them. For it had been magic.

He gathered her in his arms. And thought, when she leaves me I will have this to remember.

They swam in the turquoise sea. When the waves brought them closer and their bodies touched they smiled at each other as though they shared a special secret nobody else in the world had yet discovered. They touched each other with questing hands, and kissed warm saltwater kisses.

When they came out they ate the breakfast Yveline had fixed. As though they hadn't eaten in days they ate everything that was set before them: sliced papaya and mango, ham and eggs, croissants with butter and jam. They drank hot coffee and held hands across the table.

"I should go to work," Christian said.

"Don't. Not today. Stay with me."

"You know what will happen if I do."

"Oh, yes, I know."

"Don't look at me like that."

"I can't help it."

"I want you again."

She pushed her chair back from the table.

They were drunk in each other, besotted, insatiable. He couldn't get enough of her; she couldn't get enough of him.

In the late afternoon they showered together. He soaped her breasts, she stroked him, and they made love there with the water cascading over their bodies.

He dried her when they came out. He rested his head against her belly, holding her, marveling that it was for her as it was for him. He felt her hand upon his head, stroking his hair, and thought, how can I ever let her go?

They ate dinner at a table on his balcony. He fed her cold lobster, holding each sweet and tender piece to her lips, and once when his finger lingered she bit it gently and desire zinged through him.

"If you do that again, I'll take you here, under or on top of the table," he said, half joking, half serious.

Laurel raised an eyebrow. "Promises, promises," she said.

They drank white wine and ate sweet cherry tarts as the moon rose full and yellow in the clear night sky.

"Would you like a swim before bedtime?" he asked.

"No sharks?"

"Only me."

She rose. "I'll go change into a suit."

"I'd rather you didn't."

She looked at him. "All right," she said. "But I'll put a robe on."

They walked hand in hand down to the beach. They put their robes and towels on the sand and waded into the surf. The water was soft and as warm as the air. She had never gone swimming in the nude before and she loved the feel of the velvet-soft water caressing her skin. The waves were fluorescent, bright sparkling flashes of green where the moonbeams stroked.

They swam side by side, parallel to the shore, until at last she said, "I'm getting tired, Christian."

They headed in toward the shore, but halfway there Christian stopped her and rested his hands on her shoulders. "How tired?" he asked.

Laurel smiled. "Not that tired." She put her arms around his neck and lifted her mouth to his.

This is a little like madness, she thought when he pulled her to him. This hunger, this insatiability won't last. But for now... She felt the press of his salt-slick body against hers, his hands on her breasts.

"Touch me," he said, and her throat clogged with need.

She stroked him there in the moonlit water, and he kissed her, kissed her until she was weak with longing. Then he lifted her and held her against him and their bodies moved with the rhythm of the water.

Laurel buried her face against his throat, but as he had before he said, "Look at me. Look at me." He held her, his hands cupping her bottom, and surged against her.

Her eyes drifted closed. Oh, yes, she thought. Oh, yes.

"Tell me," he said.

"I love what you do to me," she whispered. "Oh, Christian. Christian."

"Tell me you want more."

"Yes, more."

He kissed her. He took her breath and moved against her, carried by the current and by a passion that was as vast as the sea. In that final wondrous moment it seemed to her that all of the stars in the sky merged into one great star. She cried his name, and her cry was carried on the waves until there was only the whisper of their sighs under the moonlit sky.

"Laurel?"

She looked up at him. "You're dressed," she said.

"I have to go into the office today."

She stretched a lazy cat stretch. "Don't go."

He smiled down at her. "I need the rest. "Another day like yesterday and I'll be on crutches."

"But what a way to go." She grinned up at him. "I'll miss you," she said. "And when you return I'll be waiting for you. Think about that today while you're working."

He took a step toward her. *"Fée,"* he said. "Little witch." He sat on the edge of the bed beside her and lifted her into his arms. "You know what you do to me, don't you?"

"Yes, I know," she whispered against his throat. "I know."

He gave her a small shake and kissed her. Then he cupped one breast and ran his thumb across her nipple. She moaned into his mouth and he let her go.

"You think about *that,*" he said, and headed for the door.

Laurel lay back against the pillows, her breathing rapid, her heart like a tom-tom beat in her chest. Then she smiled and said his name aloud, "Christian." And wondered how she could wait until she saw him again.

There had been a girl at Duke when he was in his junior year. Cynthia Jane Killigrew from Raleigh, North Carolina. She was a homecoming queen, a raven-haired beauty with big green eyes and a figure that made any man between sixteen and sixty stumble-footed and dry-mouthed.

They were in the same English Lit class together. The first time she smiled at him he thought it must have been his imagination. The second time it happened he smiled back. They talked. He bought her a beer at the local pub. He asked her to the spring dance and she said yes.

She wore a green dress that matched her eyes. She moved her body against his when they danced and he got so excited he danced her into a shadowed corner of the dance floor and kissed her. She answered his kiss, openmouthed, her tongue quicksilver darting to his. She grabbed his bottom and brought him hard up against her. "I can't hardly wait," she'd panted, rubbing her body against his. "Soon's the dance is over, darlin', me'n you got us some lovin' to do."

The dance was almost over when Tommy Lee Patterson cut in. He didn't like Tommy Lee and Tommy Lee didn't like him. He tapped Christian on the shoulder and said, "I'm taking her away from you." And as he'd danced away with Cynthia Jane, Christian heard him say, "I got something to tell you, sugar. Something that will knock your pretty little panties right down around your ankles."

The dance ended. The band stopped. He thought how it would be when he and Cynthia Jane were alone in his car. Or in a motel. Yes, he'd decided, they'd go to a motel. He had enough money on him. They could...

She came toward him across the dance floor, her face white, her green eyes flashing with anger. "What is it?" he said. "What—"

"Nigger!" She'd slashed him across his face with the flat of her hand. He'd stared at her, unbelieving, scarcely aware of the others who'd crowded around, of their shocked whispers, their stunned expressions. He'd looked at Cynthia Jane and Tommy Lee. Tommy Lee, his lips curled in a sneer, his eyes triumphant.

Then Christian had turned and walked out of the room.

A few of the friends he had made at Duke remained his friends. Others did not. It didn't matter. He went back to St. Dominique at the end of the term and told his grandmother that he wanted to return to France to finish his studies. She had looked at him, a sadness in her eyes he had never seen before. But she hadn't questioned him.

He returned to France that fall, and he had vowed that never again would he date a white woman. He had kept that vow until now. Until Laurel.

He didn't want to hurt her, but he was afraid that if they continued the way they were, she would be hurt. She was a beautiful and gallant woman. Like Cynthia Jane, she, too, was from the South.

But Laurel is different, he told himself. She's not like Cynthia Jane.

Still, the nagging doubt remained. He had met her mother and her sister and though they had not been aware of his race, he sensed their inborn prejudices. And he had seen a different kind of prejudice in the woman Euphemia's eyes when she looked at him and knew him to be what he was.

"I'm not my family," Laurel had said, and he believed her. But Darcie Ann and Virgie were a part of her and she loved them. How would they feel when they learned that black blood ran in his veins? How would Laurel feel if her mother turned away from her because of him?

He tried to bury himself in his work. But every once in a while during that endless day his thoughts would turn to Laurel. When they did it was not the problems that faced them he thought of, but of how she had looked this morning with her hair tumbled about her rosy face, the sheet pulled up to cover her breasts.

With the thought of her, and how it had been with them, and the knowledge that when he returned to his home this afternoon she would be waiting for him, he put aside his doubts.

He would not think about all of the tomorrows yet to come. He would think about today, and that Laurel was waiting for him. And how it would be when she was in his arms again.

Chapter Nine

"I've been staying with Christian Dumond, at his home," Laurel said when she called Eli Dorset later that day to fill him in on everything since they'd last talked. "He insisted I come here to recuperate."

"Great!" She could almost see Eli smacking his lips. "I knew I could count on you, Laurel."

"The accident wasn't really part of my plan."

"Yeah, I know. But you're using it to your advantage. That's what counts. Keep doing whatever it is you're doing, and stay in St. Dominique as long as you have to. Just make sure you have the papers for the sale of the property with you when you come back to Atlanta. Signed, sealed and delivered. Is that clear?"

"I don't know," she started to say. "I—"

"I have a call on the other line. Deal for a property I'm working on in Baja." She heard the other phone.

Heard his secretary say, "Señor Mendoza on line two." Then Dorset said, "I'm counting on you, Laurel. Don't fail me." And there was in his voice a firmness she had never heard before, and an unspoken threat that both startled and angered her.

She called her mother next. "I didn't want to tell you before," she said when Darcie Ann answered, "but I've been in an accident."

"Darlin'! What happened?"

"I had a slight concussion, Mother. That's all. Mr. Dumond has been kind enough to let me recuperate in his home. It's on the beach and—"

"The Frenchman?"

"Yes..." Laurel hesitated, then said, "Yes, Mother, the Frenchman."

"I do declare. Doesn't that just beat all. I knew from the minute I saw the two of you together there was somethin' in the air. I told Virgie. I said, 'That Christian Dumond is the most cultured man I've ever met. Wouldn't it be nice if he and Laurel got together?' " Darcie Ann gave a gay little laugh. "After all, Laurel darlin', you're almost thirty. I was eighteen when I married your daddy, and Virgie was nineteen when she married Jimmie Ray."

"And twenty when she divorced him."

"Sometimes things just don't work out." Darcie Ann sighed into the phone. "But I know they will for you, honey."

"Mother..." Laurel took a deep breath "...Mother, I'm a guest in Christian's home. That doesn't mean—"

"I know what it means, sugar." Darcie Ann laughed. "Ordinarily I wouldn't approve, but I know how serious you are about everything and that you wouldn't be there if you didn't think Christian was somebody extra special. You keep me informed, you hear? As far as I'm concerned it would be a perfect match. A Frenchman in the Merritt family. Emily Rose will absolutely die of jealousy when she finds out."

And you'll likely die of shock, Laurel thought, when she hung up the phone.

She was not sure why or how it had happened that she thought and felt differently about most things than her mother and sister did. Perhaps it had to do with her father and all the afternoons after school she had spent with him in his office at the newspaper.

He had been a great admirer of Martin Luther King, and she remembered him saying, "He's going to change the world, Laurel. We're going to be better than we were."

Some, like her mother and her sister, hadn't changed. But many others had, thanks to Dr. King and men like her father, who had believed in what he stood for.

Now, at least for a while, she could put the thought of her mother and Virgie out of her mind.

The days that followed were the happiest of Laurel's life. Her whole being, her thoughts, everything, were centered around Christian. They went out occasionally but most of the time they stayed at home, content to be with each other at the house on the beach. He left each morning at eight and returned at three. That was when the day came alive for both of them.

There was for her a special kind of joy when he got out of the car and looked up to see her standing in the doorway. Something came to life inside him then, a warmth in his eyes when he looked at her, a smile that softened the worry lines about his mouth from the pressures of the day.

They would kiss, standing there in the driveway, and after Christian had changed they'd walk on the beach, their arms around each other, barefoot in the sand. And almost always after the walk they would go back to the house, to shower together, and to make love on the big bed in his room. Their room now.

Christian did not tell her that he loved her, afraid that if he did, if the words were spoken, it would somehow change this new and still-fragile emotion between them. It was enough for now to come home and find Laurel there waiting, her arms outstretched to welcome him.

By an unspoken mutual consent they did not speak about the proposed resort. He did not tell her of the pressures being put upon him by some of St. Dominique's most influential citizens to sell the land that to him was a sacred place.

"Think of the money a resort like Dorset would bring to St. Dominique," Georges Velmont, president of the First Dominican Bank, had said.

"And of the tourism," Bernard de Fossarieu, head of the restaurateurs, as well as of the St. Dominique Tourist Association, added. "Monsieur Belain, who unfortunately no longer works with you, has told us what Dorset is offering for the land. Surely, Dumond, you must realize that you are not being realistic."

"And surely, Monsieur de Fossarieu, you must realize that the land Dorset wants to buy is the sacred burying ground of our ancestors."

"Not *my* ancestors!" De Fossarieu bristled. "As you know, Monsieur Dumond, my ancestors came from France."

And it is said on the island that your great-grandfather impregnated half the native Dominican population, Christian thought, but did not say.

There were times he wanted to tell Laurel the pressure he was under, but he was afraid if he did, she, too, would bring up the subject of the land. He didn't want that, he didn't want anything to disturb this tenuous magic they had managed to capture.

The days merged slowly one into another. He delighted in her. He found pleasure in so many things he had always taken for granted. The sunsets were more beautiful than they had ever been because he watched them with her. Food tasted better, wine was headier. They were becoming attuned to one another's moods. They could almost read each other's thoughts. He would think how good it would be to have a swim before breakfast, but before he could voice it she would say, "Why don't we have a swim?"

He sensed without her telling him when she was tired or had one of the recurring headaches she'd had since the accident. And knew that she sensed his moods, as well.

"You're tired," she would say when she greeted him. "Was it a rough day? Let me rub your shoulders, Christian. That will make you feel better." And later, when they were alone in their bed with the trade winds moving against the curtains and the scent of salt water in the air, she would say, "Rest, Christian. Let me make love to you tonight."

She would touch him with her hands and with her lips, arousing him, caressing him until it became too much. And when it did she would settle herself on him and say, "Oh, Christian. Oh, darling."

The sound of his name on her lips, the small cries she made when it became too much for her, those were the moments he lived for. He loved the touch of her hand on his skin, her smiles and her scents. Everything about her. He was bewitched, intoxicated. He was in love for the first time in his life.

But way deep down inside him was the fear... no, more than fear, it was a certainty that this could not work, that eventually they would part because they were such different people, from such different backgrounds. If they were to have children... But he closed his mind to that. It was enough for now that Laurel was with him. When she left him... No, he would not think about that, either.

Laurel had almost completely recovered from the accident. She no longer suffered from the nightmares that had plagued her in the early days after it. Her back still bothered her occasionally and when it did Christian would give her a massage that usually ended in lovemaking.

"It's part of the therapy," he always said.

"Some therapy," she would answer as she opened her arms to receive him. And later, when she lay spent beside him, she would murmur, "You missed your calling, darling. You've got wonderful hands."

And once, her face serious and sad, she said, "Don't ever do what we do with anybody else, Christian. Not our special things."

"How could I?" he said against her throat. "Not after this, Laurel. Not after you."

But still he did not say, I love you.

He took four days off so that they could sail his boat around the island. *Le Fleur du Mer* was a two-masted schooner with a galley, a dining nook, a small cabin, and a shower that held two people if they were very close together. In the afternoon, when the sky was ablaze with color, they found shaded coves, dropped anchor, and swam naked off the boat. Later, when the sky darkened, they had their dinner out on the deck and watched the moon rise over the distant mountains.

And it was on just such a night that Laurel said, "I have to start thinking about going home."

"Home?" Christian looked at her through the half darkness that almost obscured her face. "To Atlanta?"

"I have a job, Christian, but I won't have it much longer if I don't return soon."

"I don't want you to leave."

"I don't want to go."

Silence hung between them because he did not say the words that would make her stay.

"We haven't talked about the resort," she said at last. "We have to talk about it, Christian."

"Yes, I suppose we do."

"It's why I came to St. Dominique," she said.

"Is it?"

She smiled. "Not entirely."

"Is it the reason you've stayed?"

"You know better than that." Laurel reached for his hand. "You know why I've stayed, Christian." She hesitated, then, deciding it had to be said, went on. "But I do have a job and part of that job is to convince you to let us have the land we want for the resort. Eli has said he'd go to six million. I think he'll go to eight." She tightened her hand around his. "Think what that money would do for St. Dominique. You could build new schools, hospitals—"

"No!" He pulled his hand away from hers and went to stand by the rail. "There are other parcels of land," he said. "As much as I hate the thought of a resort like the kind Dorset wants to build, I might consider selling in a different location." He flexed shoulders that had gone tight with tension, and felt as though he was being pressured on all sides: by Georges Velmont, Bernard de Fossarieu, and all of the other interests who would make money if he allowed a resort the size that Dorset wanted to build to come to St. Dominique. Now he was being pressured by Laurel.

Didn't any of them understand? Didn't Velmont and de Fossarieu realize what that particular piece of land meant to the people of St. Dominique? Didn't Laurel?

He told himself as he turned away from her that she was an American, she could not be expected to understand how it had been here, how the Caribs had been slaughtered when the French first came, how the Africans had worked and died here, dreaming of the homeland they would never return to. She could not understand that the ones who had gone before were a part of him. Both Indian and African were blood of his blood.

He would fight to preserve the land that was a part of his heritage. He would fight Velmont and de Fossarieu, and yes, if he had to, he would fight Laurel.

"Christian?" She laid a hand on his arm, and felt him stiffen under her touch. "It's late," she said. "We can talk about this tomorrow. Come to bed."

He shook his head. "You go along. I'll be down in a little while."

His face was shadowed by moonlight, his eyes by an expression she could not read.

She went down to the cabin and when she had undressed she lay down and pulled the sheet up to cover her nakedness. In a little while she felt the slight tip of the boat, then the splash as his body hit the water. She started to get up because she wanted to be with him, then with a shake of her head she lay back down.

There were things about Christian that she could not understand no matter how much she loved him. Loved him... It was the first time she had allowed the thought to surface. And now that she had, she knew it was true. She loved Christian. And she didn't know what to do about it.

It was late when he came into the bed beside her. She was still awake, but because she thought he did not want her to, she did not speak, but pretended to be asleep.

It was the first night since they had become lovers that they did not make love.

* * *

When they returned to his home on Sunday night, Yveline said, "Your sister called, *monsieur.* She say it be time to take off the cast from the boy's arm."

"I'll call her," Christian said. And to Laurel, "We could drive up to Le Carbet tomorrow..." he hesitated "...if you'd like to go with me."

Laurel nodded. "Of course I would," she said.

The strain between them, difficult for her to define, still existed. She was sorry that it did, and more and more convinced that perhaps she needed to distance herself from Christian for a while. Everything between them had come so quickly, so without warning. Neither of them had had time to stop and think. They had allowed their emotions full rein, listening only to the thrumming urgencies of their bodies. But there were obstacles to any kind of a permanent relationship, questions that had to be faced.

Her mother had been delighted because Christian was French. And so he was. But the blood of the Carib Indian and African black also ran in his veins. She was Southern, steeped in the richness of tradition and love of the rich Georgia land. Her mother, a Hatfield before her marriage, came from an old Virginia family. Her great-grandparents had kept slaves; she could trace her side of the family back to Robert E. Lee.

The South had changed, but people like her mother and aunt Emily Rose hadn't changed with it. They still held to the old customs, the old beliefs. They would forever hold steadfast to the memory of the South as it had been in their forefathers' time.

Laurel had told Christian that she was not her family, and it was true. She did not think like them, she did not believe in what they believed. But they were her family. And Georgia was her home. She did not know if she could turn her back on all that she had known.

They left the beach house a little after eleven the following morning. The air was cool and fresh, and the sky was clear. Christian had the top down on his car and a calypso cassette in the tape deck.

"You're very quiet this morning," he said.

Laurel rested her hand on his thigh. "I know." She turned to look at him. "I've been thinking."

His chest tightened. "About going back to Atlanta?"

"Yes."

"You know I don't want you to go."

She leaned her head back against the seat. "But it's time I went home, Christian."

He looked straight ahead. "Yes, perhaps it is," he said.

It was a little like dying, he thought. Like losing a part of himself. He wanted to ask Laurel to stay but he couldn't bring himself to because he was afraid of what her answer would be. He did not think he could stand it if she refused.

They turned off the highway onto the road that led past the cane fields. And it came to him, as it sometimes did when he traveled here, what it had been like for the slaves who had toiled in these same fields day after day with the hot sun beating down upon their backs, filled with hopelessness and rage, longing for the families they had left behind, and for their homeland.

There were workers in the cane fields now, sons and daughters of those who had gone before, free men and women who worked an eight-hour day and went home when the day's work was through. He was a part of these people, just as he was a part of those who had gone before. That was something he didn't think Laurel would ever be able to understand. This land and these people were his. But they were not hers. They never could be.

He came around a bend in the road and saw his grandmother's house there on a rise of land. This had been his home during all of his growing-up years, and though he enjoyed his house on the beach, this was the place he had always thought of as home.

As she had before, as soon as they drove in the driveway, his grandmother hurried out to meet them. "Come in, come in," she cried after she had embraced first Laurel, then Christian. "Solange and Etienne are out on the back terrace." She linked her arm through Laurel's. "It is *un grand plaisir* to see you again, Mademoiselle Merritt. I am so happy you have decided to stay in St. Dominique for a while. You have completely recovered from your accident, yes?"

"Yes, *madame*."

"Marie. Remember?"

Laurel smiled. "Marie," she said.

Etienne ran to greet them. As he had before, Christian scooped the boy up into his arms, and when he put him down, Etienne smiled shyly at Laurel and said, *"Bonjour, mademoiselle."*

"Bonjour, Etienne." She ran her hand across the top of his head. "I hear you're going to get your cast off tomorrow."

He nodded, then, looking concerned, asked, "Do you think it will hurt, Mademoiselle Laurel?"

"I know it won't," she said. "I broke my arm when I was just about your age and when it came time to take the cast off I wondered how in the world the doctor could do it without hurting me. But he did. It didn't hurt at all, honestly."

He breathed a sigh of relief. "How did you break it?" he asked.

"I was climbing a tree," Laurel said.

"So was I!"

She grinned. "Maybe we'd both better stay out of trees from now on. Okay?"

"Okay!" He grinned back at her and, taking her hand, led her out toward the terrace. "We could go fishing instead."

"Etienne likes your friend and so do I." Marie slowed her steps, and when they were out of earshot looked up at Christian and asked, "How much do *you* like her?"

"I like her very much, *Grandmère*. Very much indeed."

"I hear a doubt in your voice, Christian. *Pourquoi?*"

"Laurel and I come from different backgrounds...." He shook his head. "It is a problem of race," he said.

"I see." Marie hesitated. "Is the problem yours or Laurel's?"

He stopped. "Well... well, hers, of course."

"I wonder." Marie shook her head. "I have seen the way she looks at you, Christian. If I am any judge of character, I would say that she cares a great deal about you.''

''And I care for her, *Grandmère.* But...'' he shrugged ''...there are obstacles that—''

''Bonjour, big brother.'' Solange hurried across the terrace to greet him, and to Laurel she said, ''I'm so glad you're here. Come, sit down. We have a while yet before lunch is ready.''

The drinks were refreshingly cool, the conversation pleasant. Laurel found Solange not only one of the most beautiful women she had ever seen, but also one of the brightest.

''My husband and I had an export business,'' Solange told her. ''I sold it after Francois died. Etienne had a difficult time after his father's death and I thought it would be better for both of us to live here with *Grandmère.*'' She smiled. ''Better for *Grandmère,* too. Having Etienne around keeps her young.''

''But what about you?'' Laurel asked. ''You don't mind being out here in the country, away from everything?'' Away from people your own age, men your own age? she wanted to add, but didn't. ''Have you ever thought of modeling? I know people in the business, in both Atlanta and New York. If you went to the States—''

Solange shook her head. ''I'm content here, Laurel. Perhaps when Etienne is older we will move back to Port-au-Mer, but I don't want to live or work in the United States. I love my island. This is where I want to be.''

Like Christian, Laurel thought. And wondered why suddenly she felt so alien, caught somewhere between the magic of this tropical island and her own Southern homeland, with a feeling that she did not quite belong to either of them.

A servant served lunch on the terrace: cream of avocado soup, a shrimp-and-crabmeat salad with crusty French bread, and finally a chocolate soufflé. Laurel, though preoccupied with her thoughts, managed to keep up with the conversation. She talked to Christian's family in her soft Southern drawl and they to her in their French-accented English that was spiced with the patois of the island.

Christian watched her, pleased that she liked his grandmother and his sister and that they liked her, and he was not surprised when after lunch his grandmother said, "Come along, Laurel. I want to show you my orchids."

The greenhouse, that Marie confessed was her pride and joy, was at the edge of a stand of date palms. "My husband built it for me the year before he died," she told Laurel. "I often come here when I'm lonely for him."

"Was he from St. Dominique?"

Marie shook her head. "No, Pierre was from France, from Provence. He was sent to St. Dominique by his family to buy a sugarcane plantation. My family owned the land he wanted to buy, but that was all we had, and because there was almost no money my father couldn't afford to hire the workers he needed to keep things going."

She led Laurel down the rows of blooming orchids. "I was seventeen when Pierre Dumond came to talk to my father. He was twenty-eight and I thought he was the most handsome man I had ever seen." She stopped in front of a low stand of purple orchids. "Pierre hired

more men to work in the fields, and he hired my father to be the overseer and me to take care of the
books.''

She smiled at Laurel. ''He had been here for two
months when he asked me to go to a dance with him.
I refused.''

''But why? If you liked him—''

''I liked him. I think by that time I had already
fallen in love with him. But I continued to refuse
him.'' Marie hesitated, then, looking at Laurel, said,
''I refused because he was white.''

Laurel stared at her. For a moment she didn't say
anything, then she said, ''But if color was not a problem for him—''

''The problem was mine, not his.'' Marie moved on
among the flowering orchids. ''Even when he told me
he loved me I turned away from him because of my
fear, and yes, because of the opposition of my family.
It took a long time, almost a year, for me to realize
that I was wrong, and to understand that it was me
Pierre loved, not the color of my skin. For him there
were no differences between us. We were a man and a
woman and we loved each other. That was all that
mattered.''

Marie turned away but not before Laurel had seen
the shine of tears in her eyes. ''He fought for me,'' she
said, ''and at last I said I would marry him.'' She held
out her left hand. ''The day we were married he put
this ring on my finger,'' she said, indicating a perfect
star sapphire surrounded by a circlet of diamonds. ''I
have never taken it off.''

''It's a beautiful ring.'' Laurel took Marie's hand
and turned it toward the light slanting in through the

overhead windows so that she could better see it. The sun reflected off the blue sapphire and the diamonds sparkled. "It's beautiful," she said again.

"As was our love," Marie said. "From the beginning of our marriage until the end we were like one person. I loved Pierre as I had never thought it possible to love, and every feeling, every emotion I felt for him he returned threefold to me. We had forty-three years together and I thank God for every one of them."

Marie raised her eyes. "Love is the essence of life," she said gently. "There are times you must fight for it, as Pierre fought for me, times too when you must fight prejudice and opposition. But it is worth the fight, because if the love is true, then it is the most important thing in the world." Marie shook her head. "I've said too much," she murmured almost to herself.

"No, *madame.*" Laurel covered the other woman's hand with her own. "I thank you for telling me."

"Christian is afraid," Marie said.

"I know."

"Sometimes, Laurel, it is up to the woman. Sometimes the woman must be braver than the man." She searched Laurel's eyes. "Do you love him?" she asked.

"Yes," Laurel said. "I love him."

"Then you must not be afraid. You must trust your heart and your love." Marie smiled. "For Christian does love you, you know. I have seen it in the way he looks at you, in the way his eyes light up when you come into a room." She rested a hand against Laurel's cheek. "Have courage," she said. "Don't be afraid to love him."

They left the greenhouse and started toward the house. Christian watched them from the terrace. His grandmother had her arm linked through Laurel's and they were smiling at each other.

Beside him, Solange said, "I like your Laurel, Christian."

His Laurel? How he wished that it were true, that by some miracle of fate they could always be together.

But he didn't believe in miracles. The day would come when he would have to let her go. And the thought of it, the thought of all the years to come without Laurel filled him with a sadness unlike anything he had ever known.

Chapter Ten

The following day the cast was removed from Etienne's arm. When it came time for him to go into the doctor's office, he looked up at Laurel, his eyes troubled, his thumb in his mouth. Very gently she took the thumb away. "It will be all right," she said. "I promise you it will be a cinch."

"A cinch?"

"Easy," she said. "It's going to be easy."

And it was. Thirty minutes later Etienne and Christian emerged from the doctor's office and a triumphant Etienne held out his arm and said, "It was a cinch, Mademoiselle Laurel."

Laurel laughed and gave him a hug. And Christian said, "I think we should have lunch before we start back to Le Carbet. How do you feel about hamburgers and french fries, Etienne?"

The place they went to was a haven for U.S. tourists who had grown tired of the French food and the native fare the island was famous for. A large group of them were sitting at one long table when Christian and Laurel entered the restaurant with Etienne.

"You two go ahead and order," Laurel said. "A cheeseburger for me, please."

"I'm going to have a *giant* burger," the little boy said.

"You can have anything you want, son." Christian put his arm around Etienne's shoulders, and with a wink in Laurel's direction, started toward the counter.

"Look at that," one of the women at the table of tourists whispered.

"He doesn't *look* black."

"More like tan."

"The boy's dark."

"But the mother is white."

"He's really quite good-looking, isn't he? You'd hardly suspect that he's... you know."

They laughed.

Laurel turned and looked at them. The whispers died. There was a shuffling of chairs when they left.

Christian and Etienne returned with two trays heaped with burgers and fries and chocolate shakes.

The cheeseburger stuck in Laurel's throat.

Etienne ate a burger and a half, all of his french fries and most of Laurel's. He chattered and laughed, and Christian laughed with him, unmindful of Laurel's silence, caught up in Etienne's pleasure in having the cast off. When they left the restaurant they started the drive back to Le Carbet. Halfway there the little boy fell asleep, and when he leaned against Laurel she put her arm around him and drew him closer.

He could be my son, she thought. If Christian and I had children . . .

"He likes you," Christian said.

"I like him."

"He was pretty good about getting the cast off."

"The doctor didn't hurt him?"

"No." Christian slowed for a curve. "How old were you when you broke your arm?"

"Fourteen."

"You should have known better than to be climbing trees."

"That's what my mother said. She thought I should have been going to dancing classes and young ladies' teas, not climbing trees."

"She was probably right."

"But I didn't want to go to dancing classes or teas. I wanted . . ." Laurel's eyebrows drew together in a thoughtful frown. "I think I wanted to deny the fact that I was growing up, Christian. I wanted to cling as long as I could to the child in me. I hated all the primping and the giggling over boys, and later I hated the balls to introduce the right class of young men to the right class of young women. I was tall for my age and most of the boys I knew came to my shoulder." She looked at him with a rueful smile. "You can't imagine what it's like when you're all legs and elbows and everybody in your family says, 'Poor Laurel is so *thin*. Isn't it too bad she doesn't look more like Virgie?'"

"I like your elbows," Christian said. "And you've got the best-looking legs this side of Venus. As for

Virgie..." He didn't like Laurel's sister, maybe because she reminded him of Cynthia Jane, maybe because she'd been so damn obvious in her come-on, but
he didn't want to offend Laurel by telling the truth.

"Virgie is pretty," he said. "But you're different."

"Different?" Laurel's eyebrows shot up but she
made no comment.

"You're the beautiful one in the family, Laurel. You
have it all. You're the kind of a woman a man..."

He hesitated. "You're the kind of a woman a man
dreams about," he finished.

It wasn't what he'd wanted to say but it would have
to do, for now.

It was late when they started back from Le Carbet.
Marie had wanted them to stay for dinner but they had
demurred, and after a cup of tea had started the return drive to the city.

They drove in companionable silence for most of
the trip, but when they neared the place overlooking
the Caribbean where Dorset wanted to build, Laurel
asked, "Can we stop for a few minutes? I'd really like
to take another look at the land."

Christian frowned. So she hadn't given up on it.
Her company wanted the land and she was determined to get it. He slowed the car and when he
stopped asked, "Would you like to get out?"

Laurel nodded. "No shoptalk. I just want to see it
again."

He got out of the car and, coming around to her
side, took her arm. "It's dark," he said. "Be careful."

They walked without speaking to the edge of the cliff. Even before they reached it they could hear the sound of the incoming tide. The water rose high and powerful and the waves smashed like the sound of thunder against the shore. White spume rose high into the air, filling the night with a sharp salt sting and the smell of the sea.

"This really is the most beautiful spot on the island," Laurel said. "I said I wouldn't talk shop and I won't. But honestly, Christian, it's the perfect place for a hotel."

"I don't want to discuss it." He turned away from her. "You know the way I feel about this."

"Yes, I know, but..." She held up her hands. "Okay, no more talk." She put her arms around his waist and brought him close to her. "Don't be angry. It's too nice a night for anger."

Christian looked out at the night-dark water. I wish you could understand, he wanted to say. I wish I had the words to tell you how I feel about this land, about this island. I wish you could see it as I do, not as a property on which to build a tourist resort, but as a place that represents all that I hold dear. This land is a part of me. It's who I am. It's sacred to me and to all of the people who feel as I do.

With all his heart, with all that he felt for her, he wanted her to understand. If she could see it the way he did, then perhaps...perhaps there was a chance for them.

He tightened his arms around her waist. "I told you about a celebration that's held here each year. It's called the Day of Commemoration, in remembrance of our ancestors."

"Yes, you told me."

"It will take place next week. I'd like you to come with me."

She tried to read the expression in his eyes but she could not.

"It would mean a great deal to me if you would," he said.

"Of course I'll come."

His arms were still around her. "You've been very quiet today." He smoothed the windblown hair from her face. "Is anything wrong?"

She thought of the conversation she'd overheard at the restaurant. "No," she said. "Nothing's wrong." She put her face against his chest. "Take me home. Take me—"

He stopped her words with a kiss, and she wanted to weep because she was filled with so many mixed emotions. Because she loved him, and because she was afraid it would never work between them.

He drew her close and she felt wrapped in the strength of his arms, and when he kissed her she felt his passion and his pain, and held him as he held her.

When at last he let her go they went arm in arm to the car.

Though he drove carefully, he kept one arm around her. Laurel leaned against him and he touched her breast. Her body throbbed with desire and she knew that soon they would be together in his bed.

And for a little while she put away her doubts and her fears.

Laurel heard the drums first, rhythmic, compelling, unlike anything she'd ever heard before. Then she saw the fires, bloodred against the darkness of the night.

Christian's face was impassive. "Come," he said when they got out of his car.

He wore a white, full-sleeved gypsylike shirt that was knotted at the waist, dark pants, sandals. His expression was remote. He looked very foreign, mysterious, alien.

They climbed the rise of the hill, and as they came up over the crest Laurel saw before her a scene that stopped the breath in her throat. It was unreal, primitive and fearful, yet vibrating with life. Men and women danced barefoot around the fires, the men stripped to the waist, the women in colorful dresses, all of them moving to the beat of the drum.

"Come closer," Christian said, and there was something in his voice she had never heard before, an expression in his eyes she had never seen. He was tense, she could tell that, but it was more. It was as though he had left the Christian she knew, that civilized man who wore expensively tailored suits, who spoke French and drove a foreign car. And another man, a man she did not know at all, had somehow taken his place.

He led her closer toward the fires. She saw the drummers squatting on the ground, drums between their knees, beating with their hands. And the dancers, men and women, their eyes half-closed, oblivious to everything except the beat of the drums, arms outstretched, bodies fluid and flowing with the rhythm, joined by a commonality of spirit in this ritual of remembrance.

The sheen of firelight glistened on naked chests. The air smelled of woodsmoke and sweat. The dancers sang in high off-key tones. The song became a chant, then a wailing cry as they moved faster and yet faster to the drums, as though evoking the spirits of those who had gone before.

A woman in a calico dress and a turban motioned Christian into the circle of dancers. He hesitated, then pulled his sandals off. The woman grabbed his hand. He looked at Laurel and held out his other hand. She shook her head and fell back into the shadows.

If any of the dancers noticed her, they paid no attention. They were caught up in this ancient ritual, some of them weeping, crying out in an ecstasy of emotion.

Christian was a part of them, dancing as they danced, singing as they sang. His bare feet beat the same rhythm, his face held the same longing. His shirt was open to the waist and she saw the shine of sweat on his chest.

More wood was thrown onto the fires. Flames shot high into the sky. Gourds were passed. Christian left the circle of dancers and someone handed him a gourd. He drank deeply then looked for her, and when he saw her he brought the gourd and held it out to her. She drank and tasted rum.

"Come dance with me," he said.

She shook her head.

"I want you to."

"I can't."

"Yes. You can."

She didn't want to be a part of this. It had nothing to do with her. It was too wild, too abandoned. She looked at him through the firelit darkness. There was something in his eyes, something hypnotic, compelling.

She kicked her shoes off. He took her hand and led her into a circle of dancers. She watched the dark bodies and tried to do what they did. Someone passed a rum-filled gourd. She drank again and so did Christian, his head tilted back, the muscles of his throat working, his skin bronzed by firelight.

Eyes closed, Laurel listened to the beat and slowly it became her beat. The hard and sensual rhythm flowed through her body as the rum flowed through her veins. She began to understand it, to move with it. She broke free of Christian's hand and raised her arms to the blackness of the night. The beat of the drum became the beat of her heart, its rhythm the rhythm of her body. She moved with it, a part of it now. Around her she heard the voices raised in their chanting cry and the sound of it filled her ears. Their cry became her own silent cry, and she understood.

The beat came faster; the dancers' movements were frantic, wildly elemental, passionate. Christian caught her shoulders and they danced facing each other, their bodies moving in unison, swaying close, then retreating, speaking a language of their own, a language of hot desire and of a need soon to be filled. There was excitement in his eyes, a look of barely repressed sensuality. His nostrils flared, his lips parted.

Blood pounding through her veins, her body felt heavy with need. She danced closer. She put her palms flat against his chest and felt his sweat and the ripple of his muscles. She ran her nails through the thatch of chest hair and heard him gasp, heard the whispered

"Fée!" before he took her hand and pulled her out of the circle back into the shadows of the palms. Gripping her shoulders, he kissed her with a passion too long held in check. She moaned into his mouth and when she did, he held her away from him.

"These are my people," he said in a voice that shook with the need to make her understand all that he was feeling. "Look at them. They're a part of me, I come from them. Look at them, Laurel, and see me. Me as I really am."

She trembled beneath his hands but he wouldn't let her go.

"I'm an island man," he said, "Indian, French..." he tightened his hands "...and African, Laurel." He looked at her for a long moment. "Do you understand that? Do you understand how different we are?"

Laurel drew a shaking breath. "Yes, Christian, I understand."

He let her go. "Would you like to go home now?"

"No, darling." She turned again and looked at the dancers. And thought of his grandmother.

Love is the essence of life, Marie Dumond had said. *If the love is true...*

She took his hand and brought it to her breast. And looked into eyes gone wide with all that he was feeling. "Christian," she whispered, and then she kissed him long and deep, and when she felt the passion in the press of his body against hers, she did not pull away but moved closer to him.

"Laurel..." The word was a whisper on his lips. "Oh, Laurel."

He took her back into his arms and held her so close she could barely breathe. "I want to make love with you," he murmured against her lips.

She felt drugged, drunk with the music and the rum, mesmerized by the glow of firelight and the flame in his eyes. She tried to answer, tried to say, "Whatever you want for as long as you want," but the words wouldn't come. All she could do was look at him and hold out her hands.

He led her past the bonfires and the dancers and the drum players to the precipice of the cliff overlooking the water. "There's a path here," he said. "Come."

With only the light from the fires they made their way down toward the sea. Then the light was gone and there was only the faint glow of the moon behind the darkness of clouds.

The sound of the surf came closer, pounding hard against the shore, as hard as the blood that pounded through their veins. From above, the drums called out across the sea to a faraway homeland.

Senses sharpened, excitement built, Christian's heart beat fast and his pace quickened.

"Wait." She sounded breathless. "I can't keep up with you."

He reached a hand up to her and brought her down beside him. He kissed her once, his mouth taking hers, tasting, consuming, frantic with the need to have her.

Her knees felt weak, not from climbing, but from a need that matched his own. Almost blindly she stumbled after him and when they were on the flat sand he drew her to him again. "Now," he said. "*Mon Dieu, now!*"

He tightened his arms around her and together they sank to their knees. He ripped his shirt off and laid her back onto the sand. He loomed above her, half-naked, his eyes narrowed with a desire that both frightened and excited her. He unfastened his belt, his trousers. She watched him pull them off. Then he was naked, standing over her, legs apart. Waiting.

She pulled her blouse over her head, then reached behind to unfasten her bra, to slip out of her skirt, her panties, her movements as fluid, as graceful as though she were in a dream.

Christian knelt on the sand beside her. Her throat clogged with desire. He said, "Touch me, Laurel. Touch me and see how much I want you."

She ran her hands along his thighs. She touched him as he had asked. His head went back, the cords of his neck tightening, and she saw the quiver of his chest and shoulder muscles.

"Oh, yes," he whispered. "Yes." And his body throbbed with a need he could no longer hold in check. He laid her against the sand, his body came over hers, then he was inside her and it was like nothing that had ever gone before.

He gave no quarter, she asked for none. He plunged deep and she lifted her body to his with a cry that tore at his very soul. This was his woman, now and forever. He wouldn't let her go, because she was a part of him.

"You belong to me," he said against her mouth.

"Yes!"

The sound of the drums from above carried to the sea. The fast, hard rhythm became their rhythm. Their bodies pulsated with it, the beat became their beat, faster and faster, abandoned, wild, consumed with heated desire.

"I can't bear it," she cried.

"Yes, you can. For me you can." He kissed her mouth. "More. I want more."

"Oh, please..."

"Not yet!"

His mouth was hungry against hers. He sucked her lips, tasting her, taking love bites, and all the while his body moved free and uninhibited against hers.

Laurel surged against him in a frenzy of indescribable feeling. "Christian," she sobbed. "Oh, please... oh, yes. Oh, darling... darling."

And it happened for him, as violent as a storm at sea. She held him with arms that never wanted to let him go, and sought his mouth to mingle her cry with his. He gasped and tightened his arms around her. He said her name over and over again, "Laurel. Laurel." And held her against his beating heart.

Long shudders ran through his body. She caressed his shoulders, whispering words of endearment, stroking him to quietness.

They held each other without speaking until she felt the splash of water over her feet and her ankles.

"Tide's coming in," Christian murmured. He roused himself to lean on one elbow and look down at her. Her hair was tousled, her eyes love-drowsed. He kissed her a saltwatery kiss as the warm sea water washed over them.

"We have to leave," he said. "Another minute and we'll be washed out to sea."

"I know." But still Laurel made no effort to rise.

The sound of the drums was muted now. She closed her eyes and felt herself drifting with the waves as though she were being carried away in the slow deep roll of the sea. In that state of half sleeping, half waking it seemed to her that carried with the sound of the waves were the voices of men and women who had stood here hundreds of years before, crying out to their native land. They had lived and died here. Perhaps they had loved here, as she and Christian had.

She knew then that he had been right, this land truly was sacred. It would be wrong to build the kind of resort Dorset wanted to build.

She remembered Hal Ginsburg's words: ". . . a hotel overlooking the sea," he had said. "Terraces down toward the water. A discotheque with enough electric guitars to be heard all the way to Jamaica."

But if there are electric guitars, how would they be able to hear the whispered voices on the waves?

Chapter Eleven

"I'd like to look at some other land sites," Laurel said the next morning at breakfast. "It was raining the day Belain drove me around the island, and we had the accident...." She shook her head. "I really don't have a clear picture of the places I saw."

Other land sites? Christian rested his fork across his plate, taking his time, wanting to be sure what Laurel meant before he answered.

He had taken her to the ceremony last night hoping against hope that she would understand what the land meant to him. She had drunk rum with him and danced with him. She had answered his passion with a passion that had set his blood on fire. But he hadn't been sure she understood the love he had for this island, for his people, and for that one particular place.

"Do you mean you've given up on the idea of the land Dorset wants?" he asked.

"Yes, Christian." She reached across the table and took his hand. "I think I know now what it means to you and to your people. I know you're right not to sell it."

"What about your boss?" he asked. "Do you think you'll be able to convince him?"

"Maybe, if I can come up with a location that's almost as good as what he wants. But if he doesn't agree..." She shrugged. "The land belongs to St. Dominique, Christian. If you don't want to sell, there isn't anything Dorset can do about it."

"What about your job?"

"It's just a job," Laurel said with a smile. "Let's not worry about it now. What are we going to do today?"

"Do you have to ask?"

He lifted her hand to his lips. She felt the heat of his tongue against her skin of her palm and a flame curled and grew deep within her. He rubbed his thumb across her lips. She licked it and saw the rise of passion in his eyes.

"Christian..."

He shook his head, but a slow smile curved the corners of his mouth. "Eat your breakfast," he said. "And afterward..." He let the word hang in the air. "Afterward we'll drive around the island and you can have a look at other parcels of land. All right?"

"All right," she said, and knew what would happen before the afterward.

* * *

It was a perfect Caribbean day. The month was June and the air was filled with summer sunshine and summer scents. The sea was flat and calm, a perfect turquoise dotted with the white sails of small boats and the more tattered sails of the fishing boats. There were other fishermen along the shore, some who waded hip deep into the waves and cast out nets that were butterfly yellow against the clear blue sky.

They passed women walking barefoot along the road, carrying baskets of fruit on their heads, and Christian said, "Fruit is more plentiful on this side of the island. There are hundreds of acres of mangoes and papaya, pineapple and bananas. We export fruit and fish to France and Germany, as well as to the United States, of course, but our main resources come from sugarcane. St. Dominique rum is popular all over Europe."

"I can see why." Laurel grinned at him. "It's potent stuff, Monsieur Dumond. It makes a lady lose her head and do things she's never dreamed of doing."

"Does the lady mind?"

"What do you think?" She put an arm up over the back of his seat and began to caress his neck. How to tell him? How to express in words all that she had felt last night during the ceremony of remembrance for those who had gone before? She had sensed a throbbing vitality of life, and for a brief time she had been part of the universe, the land, and of the deep and abiding sea. It had come to her when she lay naked in Christian's arms with the sea water splashing over them and the pounding beat of the drums from above, how very far she was from everything she had ever known. There had been no restraints of society to hold her back. She had let herself go with total abandon, to love and be loved.

The experience had been unlike anything she had ever known or hoped to know again. For that space of time she had been free, no longer bound to the rules of the more restricted world she had grown up with.

This island, and Christian, had changed her. Because of him she would look at the world with a different awareness.

Christian stopped the car and pointed to a stretch of land that ran from the sea up to the edge of the mountains. "This is for sale," he said. "It's smaller than the other site but it's right on the beach and that's an advantage."

"It certainly is." Laurel got out of the car and walked beside Christian. "The view is different, not as spectacular as the other, but it's still good." She took out her notebook. "How many acres?" she asked.

"Ten."

"Asking price?"

"Three million five."

Laurel nodded. "I like it, Christian. Maybe Eli will, too."

"There's another place higher up that you should look at." He took her arm and led her back to the car. "It's in the mountains, with a pretty good view of the sea."

It was a beautiful piece of land set in a junglelike atmosphere where bamboo, thatch palms, saw palmettos and mahogany trees grew. There were mango trees too, along with brilliantly colored bougainvillea and wild orchids. Sunlight filtered through the trees and butterflies of every hue flitted and fluttered.

"It would be harder to build here," Christian said. "Construction costs would be higher. And you're farther away from the beach."

"There could be some kind of transportation down to it, if that's what people wanted. And a swimming pool up here. A lot of the trees and underbrush would have to be cleared but it could be done." She turned to him. "I like it, Christian. Have you got a price?"

"Not a definite one," he said. "But it would be less than the other because it's away from the beach."

They saw one more piece of property near the village of Saint Esprit. It was closer to the sea but farther from the mountains. Laurel didn't like it as much as she had the first two properties, but she duly made note of it so that when she called Eli she would have three alternate sites to suggest.

She wasn't sure what he would say when she told him she agreed with Christian about the land he wanted, but perhaps his anger would be muted if she quickly suggested these other properties.

Eli liked her and he respected her work. But he had a temper that she had seen flare like a rocket when he was crossed. More than one executive had been fired for disagreeing with him. He was as tough as they came, which was probably why he had come as far as he had. He wouldn't like her crossing him, but she would. She would do whatever she had to do to stand by Christian.

They heard the music even before they reached the village of Saint Esprit.

"Every village celebrates The Day of Commemoration in their own way," Christian said. "I guess they're still celebrating here." He smiled at her. "Are you up to it?"

"After last night I'm up to anything," she answered. "But no more rum, okay?"

"Pourquoi pas, ma chère?" He put his arm around her and drew her closer. "A little rum does wonderful things for you."

"And for you," she said with a laugh.

They drove into the village and as they grew closer they heard the sound of the beguine, that vigorous rumbalike music that was so popular in this part of the Caribbean.

The band played in a kiosk in the center of the town square that was filled with people of all ages. Women wore bright silk scarves and skirts, embroidered bodices and petticoats, and hibiscus blossoms in their hair. Little girls were dressed like their mothers, the men and boys in flowered pants and shirts.

"Do you want to stop?" Christian asked.

"Of course."

"All right, come on." He reached for her hand. "Let's dance."

Laurel looked toward the women. "Wait here for me," she said. "I'll be right back." And with a wave of her hand she disappeared through the crowd gathered at the edge of the square watching the dancers.

Fifteen minutes later she emerged from the town's one store dressed in a bright red skirt and a white blouse embroidered with a rainbow of colors. A hint of embroidered petticoat showed beneath the skirt. Her hair was tied back with a multicolored silk scarf.

"Alors, monsieur," she said when she reached Christian, "Are you ready for ze dance?"

His gray eyes sparkled with laughter. He said, *"Mais oui, mademoiselle,"* and holding both her hands, held her away from him so that he could look at her. *"Bon!* You look *merveilleuse."* He took the package that held the clothes she had worn and put it in the car, and, taking her hand, led her toward the dancers.

Two little girls stared up at Laurel openmouthed, obviously wondering what this strange lady was doing in their village. A man winked at her and the woman next to him yanked so hard on his hand that he almost lost his balance. A few of the women smiled politely, others frowned.

But little by little it began to change. The circle divided into couples. Laurel and Christian danced together, then an elderly man with a curly white beard tapped Christian on the shoulder and asked if Laurel would dance with him. She did, while Christian bowed to one of the little girls and began to dance with her.

The music grew louder, the beat more frantic. Laurel danced with other men, Christian with other women. Then they danced with each other. By the time the circle reformed the attitude had changed. One of the women said, "Here, you must take these," and put a string of bright orange beads over Laurel's head.

When at last the dancing stopped everyone headed for the shade of the banyan trees. The men and women were friendlier now, the children still curious. They gathered around Laurel, touching her hair, asking her name and where she came from. She answered as best she could in what little French she had, and when they giggled over her accent she giggled right back. A little boy in diapers toddled over to see what was going on. Halfway there he wobbled and fell. When he started to cry Laurel picked him up and put him on her lap.

She began to sing, in a sweetly off-key voice,

"Hush little baby, don't you cry.
Mama's gonna sing you a lullaby..."

The child looked up at her and stopped crying. People around her smiled and a woman asked, "You have babies too, *madame?*"

Laurel shook her head. "I'm not married," she said.

"That not be necessary to having babies," another woman said, and all of them laughed.

"You like children so you should have many. Nine or ten at least." The boy's mother smiled at Laurel. "You would be a nice mother, I think."

A nice mother.

The child's hands were dark against the whiteness of her skin. He put one of the bright orange beads in his mouth and Laurel said, "No, sweetheart, it might break," and, taking a gold link bracelet off her wrist, gave him that to play with instead.

Careful not to show all that he was feeling, Christian watched her with a sudden feeling of panic. He and Laurel had taken no precautions. He had not considered the consequences of their lovemaking and he should have. It had been his responsibility as well as Laurel's to make sure that she was protected.

His palms grew damp. Was Laurel on the Pill? He should have asked. It was stupid of him not to have asked.

The music began again and he said, "It will be dark in a little while. We'd better start back."

"Yes, all right." She handed the boy to his mother, but when she tried to return the beads to the woman who had given them to her, the woman shook her head and said, "They be for you, sister."

Sister. Yes, she had felt it last night in the circle of women around the fire, and again today when she and the other women had gathered beneath the trees to talk of children. It was a kinship that went beyond blood; the spirit of the universal female.

She took her bracelet from the child and handed it to the woman who had given her the beads, and when she looked into the woman's eyes she saw an understanding of heart she had never felt before.

"There's something I have to ask you," Christian said. "I should have asked before but I didn't think of it." He hesitated because this was more difficult than he'd thought it would be. "We haven't taken any precautions." He cleared his throat. "Are you on the Pill?"

For a moment Laurel didn't answer, and when she did she said, "Stop the car for a moment, Christian."

Mon Dieu, he thought. What if...? He pulled the car to the side of the road and stopped.

Laurel turned on the seat to face him. "Yes," she said, "I'm on the Pill. I hadn't been but I went on it before I came to St. Dominique."

"But..." He shook his head, surprised and yes, just a little shocked.

"That was precipitous of me and it embarrasses me to tell you." She put her hand over his. "I'm not a promiscuous woman, Christian. I didn't plan that we would be as we are. But I think I knew from the very first time you kissed me that something would happen between us. So yes, I've been taking the Pill."

"Thank God!"

She wasn't sure why that hurt but it did. Would it be so awful if she hadn't been taking precautions? If she were pregnant? She looked at him, then away. "Don't worry," she said. "I'm not pregnant. But even if I were, it would be my problem, not yours."

"I didn't mean—"

"I know what you meant," she said, cutting him off.

He put his arms around her and though she resisted he pulled her close. "Don't be angry that I asked," he murmured against her hair.

"I'm not angry." She looked up at him. "Would you hate it if I were pregnant?"

"It wouldn't be good for you."

"I'm twenty-nine. Why wouldn't it be?"

"You know damn well why it wouldn't." He held Laurel away from him. A maelstrom of feelings was churning inside him: so many doubts, so many fears. "I haven't said the words," he said at last. "But I think you know the way I feel about you. How much I care for you. These last few weeks, being with you, making love with you..." For a moment emotion choked him and he couldn't go on. "I'm an island man, Laurel. St. Dominique is my home. I don't want to live anywhere else. You're from a different background, a different culture." He touched her face, and then he let her go and put both of his hands on the steering wheel.

"I think..." She stopped then, gaining courage, said, "I think that it's wrong not to trust what you feel, Christian. Because love..." There, she'd dared to say the word and now that she had, she could say the rest of what she was feeling. "Love is the best there is of life. To turn your back on love once you have found it would be like laughing in the face of the gods. Like saying, 'Take back your gift. I have no need of it.'"

"Laurel—"

She put a finger against his lips. "We don't have to talk about it now, Christian. Let's just be like we were. Let's take the gift the gods have given us for as long as we can. If I should leave you, or you should leave me, we'll have had this." She took her finger away and kissed him. "And *this* is a pretty good thing to have."

He wanted to tell her that he loved her and that he would never let her go. He wanted to tell her so many things.

He started the car. She rested her head against his shoulder, but they didn't speak all the way back to his home.

"There be two calls for you." Yveline handed Laurel two slips of paper. "I say I don't know when you be back. The man—he the one who call first—he sounded mean. The lady was nice but she talked funny."

"Mama," Laurel said.

"And your boss." Christian opened the door to the library. "Go ahead and make your calls. I'll fix a couple of drinks and meet you out on the terrace when you're through. Good luck."

Her smile was rueful. "I have a feeling I'm going to need it," she said.

She called Eli first. His secretary said, "Oh, Miss Merritt. Mr. Dorset's been trying to call you all day. I'll put you right through."

She heard him pick up the phone. He said, "Laurel?" and she knew he was upset.

"Hi, Eli," she said. "How're things in Atlanta?"

"Where in the hell have you been? I've been trying to call all day."

"I'm sorry. Actually, Eli, I was out looking—"

"Why haven't I heard from you? What's going on? I thought by now you'd have the deal wrapped up. Is it wrapped up, and if it isn't, I want to know why. Well? Well?"

"The deal isn't wrapped up," Laurel said as calmly as she could. "Mr. Dumond still refuses to let go of the property."

"It was your job to convince him. That's why I sent you to St. Dominique."

"I did my best, Eli, but now that I've been here I can understand Christian's reason for not wanting to sell. It—"

"What?" It was an enraged roar. "What in the hell are you talking about?"

"The land is special to the people of St. Dominique. It's part of their past, of their culture. It's a sacred place. A—"

"A sacred place!" She heard a thud, knew he was pounding his desk, and held the phone away from her ear.

"I sent you to the island to do a job," he roared. "And you're going to tell me the land I want to buy is a sacred place! Horse hockey!"

He was breathing hard. She knew that by now his face would be beet red.

"I've been in touch with a man by the name of Georges Velmont and he's all for the resort," he said. "If Dumond won't do business with us, then by God I'll find somebody who will."

"Listen . . ." Laurel took a deep breath. "I looked at three other properties today. Two of them would be wonderful for a Dorset resort. The first was right on the beach, the other was up in the mountains with a great view of the Caribbean. Either one of them—"

"Is not what I want," Eli shouted. "I sent you to St. Dominique for the express purpose of convincing Dumond to sell that place over the sea to us. You haven't done it, so I'm sending Victor Reiger. He can deal with Velmont. Meantime I want you to get your fanny back to Atlanta."

"It would be a mistake to send Reiger," Laurel said as calmly as she could. "And as for my fanny, Eli, I will get it back to Atlanta when I damn well please."

She put the phone down, stopping his sputtered oath in midair. And knew she'd probably just blown the best job she'd ever had.

For a few minutes she sat with her hand on the phone, knowing she should call her mother but not quite up to it. First she had to tell Christian about Victor Reiger.

He was out on the terrace in a chair facing the sea, but he turned when he heard her and said, "Did you make your calls?"

"One of them. I'll call my mother later."

He handed her a rum punch. "It didn't go well with your boss?"

"No, Christian." She took a sip of her drink. "He's sending our head of international sales to St. Dominique. He said he'd been in touch with a man by the name of Velmont. Georges Velmont."

Christian swore under his breath.

"Who is he?"

"President of the First Dominican Bank. He'd sell his own mother to get a resort like Dorset's on the island. He wields a lot of influence on this island because his wife is President Bazaine's sister." Christian got up and went to stand at the edge of the terrace, looking out toward the sea. "I'll try to see Bazaine tomorrow."

"Tell him I'll do everything I can to convince Reiger—that's the man Eli is sending—to at least look at the places we've seen today. Victor's a good judge of land. Once he sees either of the two properties, he might change his mind." She touched Christian's sleeve. "I feel like this is my fault," she said. "If I hadn't come to St. Dominique—"

"Somebody else would have." He turned and, resting his hands on her shoulders, said, "I'm glad it was you who came, Laurel. But what about your job? You were supposed to convince me to sell and you haven't done that. Now your boss is sending someone else. How does that affect you?"

"Eli is upset, Christian. But he likes me and he's trusted my opinion on other projects. Once he cools down it might be all right. If it isn't . . ." she shrugged ". . . I'm good at what I do. I can always get another job."

Even after Eli spreads the word all over Atlanta that you fumbled the ball? a voice inside her head questioned. He'd try to have her blackballed. He'd done it before with other employees. Her only hope was to try to convince Reiger to at least look at the other two properties. But Reiger didn't like her. He hadn't liked her speaking out at business meetings or suggesting new projects. Once he'd said, "You think you're the fair-haired girl around here, don't you?"

"Woman," she'd said. "The word is woman, Victor."

A year ago she and Victor had been sent to upstate New York to look over a project Eli had been interested in. They'd gone out to dinner with the local money people and Victor had too much to drink. When they went back to the hotel he'd tried to push his way into her room. He'd grabbed her arm. She had tried to get away from him and when he wouldn't let her go she'd kicked him. When a bellman started down the hall toward them she had called out and asked him to see Victor to his room.

Since then, Victor had done everything he could to block any suggestions she came up with. He'd wanted to be the one to come to St. Dominique and now he was coming. It would take an act of God or the St. Dominican congress to convince him even to look at the other properties.

She didn't want Christian to know how precarious her situation was. "Eli and I have had problems before," she said. "I don't think I need to worry about my job."

They finished their drinks and had dinner. Afterward they went for a walk on the beach and it was almost midnight by the time they came back to the house.

"I'm too tired to call my mother tonight," Laurel said when they were getting ready for bed. "I'll call her in the morning."

All she wanted to do was sleep, to block out all thought, and put off until tomorrow the things she didn't want to think about tonight: her mother, her job, and the relief on Christian's face when she'd told him she was on the Pill.

She thought that he loved her, but she knew now that even if he asked her to marry him—and that was a very big if—he did not want children. Could she, even for Christian, give up her lifelong dream that someday she would marry and have babies?

Now more than ever that was what she wanted: a little boy who looked like Christian, a little girl who might be as beautiful as his sister Solange.

Other thoughts. Christian had said he was an island man. Could she be an island woman?

And thoughts of home came to her, memories of a Georgia springtime, the warm heavy scents of summer, and the clear crisp autumns when the leaves turned golden in the sun. She would give up the land she loved with a gladness of heart to be with Christian. If he wanted her.

She felt a stab of pain behind her eyes and lay back against the pillows.

"Headache?" Christian asked.

"Yes." She reached her hand up to him. "Sorry," she murmured. "Sorry."

He came in beside her and gathered her into his arms. "Rest, my darling," he said. And held her until she slept.

Chapter Twelve

Christian was in the shower the next morning when the phone call came in.

"Darlin'!" Darcie Ann said when Laurel answered. "I haven't heard from you in days. How are you? How's everything on that beautiful tropical island, and how's your handsome Frenchman? Has he popped the question yet?"

"Christian is fine, Mother."

"And?"

"We haven't discussed marriage."

"What's holding him back?" Laurel's mother chuckled. "I've never yet met a man a Merritt woman couldn't twist around her little finger when she set her mind to it. Honeysuckle and roses, baby. Remember that. It works every time."

Laurel clutched the phone against her cheek and waited a moment before she said, "How's Virgie?"

"Bored, honey. Just bored out of her ever-lovin' mind."

"Maybe if she got a job, she wouldn't be bored."

"A job?" Darcie Ann laughed. "Virgie wasn't cut out for work, honey. She needs a man to keep her happy."

Men, Laurel thought, but said, "Is she still seeing Boone Lockwood?"

"Boone! That shameful rascal went to his cousin Mary Beth's wedding in Birmingham last month. Mary Beth introduced him to a friend of hers and a week later Boone up and married her. Virgie is absolutely heartbroken, Laurel. She just has to get away. So we've decided to come to St. Dominique."

"Come to... You're coming to St. Dominique?"

"That's why I called you, darlin'. Poor little Virgie is just fading away with sorrow, so day before yesterday I said, 'Why don't we get on a plane and go visit Laurel?' And she perked right up."

"When..." Laurel wet her lips. "When are you coming, Mother?"

"The end of the week. You could make us a hotel reservation or we could—"

"Yes, I'll make a reservation," Laurel said quickly. "There's a nice hotel right on the beach, the Place Royale. I know you and Virgie will like it."

"Well, all right. I reckon that'll have to do. Anyway, I can't wait to see you and that good-looking Frenchman. And don't you worry, baby. I'll talk some sense into him. I consider myself real broad-minded but I don't approve of my little girl living in sin. I'm planning on having a heart-to-heart talk with Christian as soon as we get there."

"Mother..." Laurel could feel last night's headache come pounding back. "I wouldn't like that, Mother," she said.

"But it's for your own good, darlin'. Now don't you worry about a thing. Virgie and I will be there on Saturday. You take care, hear?"

Laurel put the phone down and pressed her fingertips against her forehead. Her mother and sister were coming to St. Dominique and there wasn't anything she could do to keep them away, aside from disclaiming all family ties. As far as Christian was concerned she would tell her mother that she was not to bring up the subject of marriage. It was her affair and she would handle it. But God, she wished she didn't have to cope with her mother and Virgie right now.

She was sitting on the edge of the bed when Christian came out of the shower. "Did I hear the phone?" he asked.

Laurel nodded. "Mother called."

"Oh? How is she?"

"Fine." Laurel looked at him. "She and Virgie are flying to St. Dominique on Saturday."

"This Saturday?"

She nodded. "I'll make a reservation for them at the Place Royale."

"They could stay here if you'd like them to."

"No," she said quickly. "The hotel is fine."

"How long are they staying?"

"Mother didn't say."

Her brow was furrowed and he knew the headache had come back. "You'll like having them here," he said. "It will be fun for you."

"Perhaps."

"I've got to get ready for the office. Rest for a while. I'll have Yveline bring you in a tray."

The phone rang again. Christian picked it up, listened and said, "Yes, just a moment." And to Laurel he said, "It's Atlanta."

She looked at him, rolled her eyes heavenward, and took the phone.

"Laurel? Victor Reiger here. I'm flying to St. Dominique today. My plane gets in at noon. Please meet me."

She pinched the skin between her eyes. "All right, Victor."

"You can fill me in on what you have or haven't done. I have an appointment with Georges Velmont and a man by the name of Bernard de Fossarieu at three. They're agreeable to the sale even if your Mr. Dumond isn't."

"Monsieur Dumond is Minister of Commerce and Trade in St. Dominique—"

"And I fully intend going over his head, directly to the president if necessary."

"Dammit, Victor—"

"Noon today," he said. "Figure on lunch so that we can talk."

"I take it that wasn't good news," Christian said when she hung up.

"It was Victor Reiger. He's arriving at noon today and wants me to meet him."

"You should have told him you didn't feel well."

"I'll be all right. A couple of aspirin..." Laurel rubbed her temples. "It's part of my job," she said. "I don't have any choice."

"I can send one of my men to pick him up."

"No, Christian, I'd better do it." She hesitated. "He has an appointment at three with Velmont and a man by the name of de...?" She shook her head. "I don't remember."

"De Fossarieu," Christian said, and swore. He strode to the closet and took out a conservative business suit. "I've got to see President Bazaine before Reiger gets to them. Dammit to hell!" He took a steadying breath. "I'll send a car for you at eleven. The driver will take you to the airport and anywhere else you want to go." He bent to kiss her forehead. "I'm sorry about all of this, Laurel, and sorry that you have to be involved."

"But I am involved, Christian. And believe me, I'll do everything I can to convince Victor that the land Dorset wants won't do." She reached for his hand. "It's going to be all right. Try not to worry."

He forced a smile. "I'll see you tonight. Would you like to invite Reiger for dinner?"

"Lord, no! I'm having lunch with him. That's enough!"

"If you change your mind and decide to arrange something, it will be all right with me." He headed for the door. "I'll call you later," he said. With a grin he added, "Have a nice day," and laughed when she threw her bedroom slipper at him.

But Christian's laughter died when he got in his car and headed toward the city. It worried him that Dorset was sending Victor Reiger to St. Dominique, and that Reiger was seeing Georges Velmont and de Fossarieu this afternoon.

Velmont, the son of wealthy bankers in Marseilles, had come to St. Dominique ten years before to open a branch office. From the very beginning he had pandered to the political and monied interests on the island. He cared nothing for the history of the land because it wasn't a part of him. He was French; he had no interest in St. Dominique except for the money it brought into his banking family's coffers.

As for Bernard de Fossarieu, he was a money-grubbing bastard. Ashamed of his blood and of his heritage, he spent as much time as he could away from St. Dominique. Neither he nor Velmont felt any loyalty to the island.

But President Bazaine did. If he could get to him before the other two saw Victor Reiger, he had a chance. The office could wait; he had to see the president.

Victor Reiger was the first one off the plane. A bull-like man with massive shoulders and chest, his pale complexion and blond-white hair gave him a Germanic look. At first glance he was attractive, but when you looked into his almost colorless eyes and saw the coldness and the uncompromising hardness there, you knew he was not a man to trifle with.

He climbed down the steps of the plane wearing a white, unwrinkled suit, and pushed his way through the ground crew toward the terminal.

"Damn!" he said by way of greeting. "Is it always this hot? How do you stand it?"

"Quite well," Laurel answered. "I find the summer here much cooler than Atlanta." Then, making an effort to be civil, she said, "I have a car waiting, Victor. Why don't we get your luggage and go to the hotel."

"I have everything I need." He indicated his carry-on bag. "Let's get going."

She led the way out of the terminal to the car Christian had sent to pick her up. The driver got out to open the door; Reiger got in without acknowledging him. At the hotel he ordered a bellman to take his bag up to his suite, and, taking Laurel's arm, led her toward the bar.

"Something tall and cold," he told the waitress. And to Laurel he said, "You?"

"I'll just have an iced tea."

He nodded and when the waitress left to get their drinks he gave Laurel an appraising look. "What have you done to yourself?"

"What do you mean?"

"You look sensational." He hitched his chair closer. "You always were a damned good-looking woman, but now you're a knockout. Maybe it's the tan. Maybe it's Dumond." His smile was slyly insinuating. "Maybe the Frenchman's got a technique I need to hear about."

Laurel clenched her teeth to bite back a reply. Because she knew she wouldn't be able to help Christian if she were unpleasant to Victor, she made herself say, "I had to rest a lot after the accident. I really haven't been doing much of anything, just some swimming and beach walking."

"It sure as hell agrees with you."

The waitress brought the drinks. He took a long pull of his before he said, "All right. Let's get down to business. What about Dumond? Why won't he agree to letting us have the land? And why haven't you convinced him that he should?"

Laurel put her hands around her glass of tea. She did not think Victor would understand, but she had to try. "There's a cemetery on the land," she said. "A burial place for the Carib Indians who lived here before the French came, and for the African slaves who came later. To most of the people in St. Dominique it's a sacred and holy place."

Victor's expletive was to the point.

Her mouth tightened but, ignoring the obscenity, she forced herself to go on. "Once a year there's a celebration, Victor. I went to it because I wanted to see and understand why Christian objected to his government's letting us have it."

Fighting desperately to find the words that would make Victor Reiger know how important this land was to the people of St. Dominique, she said, "Columbus discovered the island in 1493. He was driven off by the Carib Indians but two hundred years later a Frenchman by the name of Francois Duvalier took possession of St. Dominique in the name of France. The Caribs fought the takeover for a long time but finally they were driven back into the jungles and most of them were killed off."

"I know about all that crap." Victor downed half his drink and signaled for the waitress. "But what in the hell does it have to do with our building a resort?"

Laurel leaned forward, her face intent, determined to make him understand. "The land belongs to the people who lived and fought and died here, Victor. And to the people who came after them."

For a moment Reiger didn't speak. Then he smiled and shook his head. "Amen and praise the Lord if you don't sound just like a Georgia preacher." He patted Laurel's knee. "You been shacking up with the Frenchman, babe? Listening to him preach the gospel of *l'amour toujours* at night while he dishes out a lot of hogwash about the land being sacred?"

Laurel shoved her chair back, but before she could rise Victor gripped her wrist. "Okay, okay," he said placatingly. "Don't get your feathers ruffled."

It took every ounce of Laurel's will, and the knowledge of what the land meant to Christian, for her not to tell Victor Reiger to go to hell.

"I had a couple of belts on the plane and maybe they hit me. So I apologize, okay?" He slapped some money on the table. "C'mon," he said. "Let's have lunch."

They went to the outside terrace of the hotel. He ordered Bloody Marys for both of them. There were a lot of tourists, as well as vacationing St. Dominicans at the hotel, and the pool area was crowded. Victor ogled every woman between fifteen and fifty, many in skimpy bikinis, some of them topless.

"I could get to like it here," he said when he bit into a piece of lobster. "Been a month of Sundays since I've had me some real fun." He winked at Laurel. "Maybe it's time I changed my luck."

The food stuck in her throat. Ignoring his comment, she said, "I looked at three other properties yesterday, Victor. Two of them are excellent, one is spectacular. You really ought to see them. There probably isn't time today but we could do it in the morning."

Victor shook his head. "Eli wants the land on the cliff overlooking the ocean," he said. "No point in even looking at anything else." He stabbed a piece of lobster with his fork. "Stupid of you to try to fight him on this, Laurel. Might just cost you your job."

"I realize that, Victor. But—"

"No buts, babe. Eli's mad as hell and I don't blame him. He sent you here to convince Dumond to let us have the land. Instead you moved in with Dumond, which would have been okay if you'd convinced him to let us have the land. But you didn't, pally. I'm afraid you've blown your job."

A drizzle of melted butter ran down his chin. He wiped it away with the back of his hand. "I might be able to help you get it back, though," he said.

Laurel waited.

He put his fork down. "You play my game and I'll play yours."

"Just what is your game, Victor?" she asked.

"A little of what the British call slap and tickle." He laughed. "Like kids say, 'I'll show you mine if you'll show me yours.'" The laughter died. "I can save your hide, Laurel, but I want a piece of yours in return. A couple of days in the sack just might convince me to help you."

Laurel didn't answer. She pushed her chair back and, rising, picked up her as yet untouched Bloody Mary, walked around to his side of the table, and slowly poured it over Victor Reiger's head.

Then, without a word, ignoring the stares and gasps of the people at the nearby tables, she walked across the terrace and out of the hotel.

"How did it go with Reiger?" Christian asked when he came home late that afternoon.

"It didn't," Laurel said.

"Oh?" He raised an eyebrow. "What happened?"

She shrugged. "He had a few drinks, we had lunch and I left."

"That's all?"

She didn't want to tell him her job was in jeopardy or about what Victor had said. She had never seen Christian angry but she had a feeling that if she told him what had happened, he might do the other man bodily harm. She didn't want that. Christian had enough to worry about; he didn't need this extra annoyance.

"That's all," she said. "What about you? Were you able to see the president?"

Christian shook his head. "He'd gone to Martinique for the day. He'll be back tomorrow and I'll try to see him then." He looked at her, his expression troubled, questioning. "Did you and Reiger have words?" he asked. "How did you leave him?"

"With a Bloody Mary running over his head," Laurel answered before she thought. And remembering how Victor had looked with tomato juice running down his face and the stalk of celery stuck in his breast pocket, she started to laugh. "All over his white suit," she gasped between bouts of laughter. "You should have seen him. Victor the immaculate, tomato juice all over his clean white suit."

She thought of the small carry-on case he had with him and knew that he probably hadn't brought another suit. That made her laugh even harder. "I don't think..." The laughter began to turn to tears. Near hysteria, she managed to say, "I don't think he kept his appointment with Monsieur Velmont and Monsieur de Whatever-his-name-is this afternoon."

Christian took hold of her shoulders. "Take it easy," he said. "Okay? Okay, Laurel?"

She hiccuped. "O-okay," she murmured.

"Tell me what happened."

Another laugh bubbled to the surface and she put her fingers over her mouth to stem it. "I poured my drink over his head," she said.

He gave her a gentle shake. "Why?"

"Because..." She shook her head. "It isn't important," she said.

"Tell me why, Laurel."

"It...it was about Eli. About my job. I didn't tell you, but last night I hung up on Eli. That probably cost me my job. Today Victor offered to help me get it back." She stopped, reluctant to go on.

"In exchange for what?"

"Me," she said. "For a couple of days."

Without thinking, Christian tightened his grip on her shoulders. *"Merde!"* he exploded and, letting her go, headed for the door.

"No," she cried, going after him. "He isn't worth it. Please, Christian, it doesn't matter. I shouldn't have told you. Let it go. Please, just let it go." She took hold of his arm. "It's been a lousy day," she said. "Let's take a walk on the beach and maybe have a swim." She looked up at him. "Please. Stay here with me."

A muscle in his jaw jumped and he hesitated. "All right," he said at last. "I'll change. We'll have that walk."

But Christian knew that before Victor Reiger left St. Dominique he would pay him a visit at the Place Royale Hotel. They would have a heart-to-heart talk, and he would give Reiger a lesson in good manners. A lesson he would not soon forget.

She dreamed of home. Of girls in white summer dresses and young men in pale frock coats. Of church picnics and barbecues, and stolen moonlight kisses under willow trees.

In her dream she was very young, still in her teens. It was dusk, that lovely Southern time of day when everything stills, when the air is warm and the sky turns summer gold.

She walked with a young man whose face she couldn't quite discern. And she was wearing a hoop-skirted gown of green taffeta that rustled like dried leaves every time she took a step.

"Look there," the young man said, and she saw before her the most beautiful antebellum home she had ever seen. There were flickering lights in every window, and as she listened she heard music.

"How beautiful," she said, but when she turned to the young man he was no longer there and she was alone under the willow trees.

She went closer. She could hear the sound of banjos playing and muted voices singing:

"I wish I was in the land of cotton..."

The scent of cape jasmine drifted on the night air, the faintest whisper of wind stirred the leaves of the willows. Suddenly an overwhelming sense of sadness, of nostalgia for a way of life that had been and was no more, filled her. She wanted to return to the beauty and the grandeur of that lost life: the house, the land and the music, all so heartbreakingly beautiful.

But as she started toward the house, a fog rolled up from the ground. The flickering lights of the house began to dim. The music stopped, the voices faded.

She moved closer and saw that the white pillars surrounding the veranda were chipped and crumbling. The windows were broken, the front door sagged.

The fog came closer, thicker. It surrounded the house. She couldn't see. Couldn't...

"Oh, no," she whispered. "It's too beautiful.... Don't let it go away. Don't..."

"Laurel?" A voice called to her through the fog. "Laurel?"

She opened her eyes and saw Christian. "I...I think I was dreaming," she said.

"Yes, dear." He tried to put his arms around her but she pulled away from him and sat up. "That's it!" she said. "Of course!"

"Of course what?"

"Historic conservancy."

He smiled. "Darling, you're still dreaming."

She looked at him. "The preservation law," she said.

"What are you talking about?"

"When they tried to tear down the antebellum homes in Georgia, and in Mississippi and Louisiana, the different historical societies stopped them because the homes were historical sites. It was the same in California with the Victorian houses. They were declared protected under some kind of conservancy law."

Her eyes shone with excitement. "Don't you see? It could be the same for the land that Dorset wants. The cemetery is there, it's a historic site." She gripped his arms. "If there is such a law, then Dorset couldn't touch it, not for any amount of money."

"Mon Dieu!" Christian switched on the bedside lamp and stared at her. "Why didn't I think of it?"

"Is there such a law?"

"I don't know. I don't think so. But if there isn't, I can damn well try to get one passed."

He put his arms around her. His face was jubilant. "How did I manage it?" he asked with a shake of his head.

"Manage what?"

"To find a woman like you?" He cupped her face between his hands and kissed her. "Beauty and brains," he said. "And the best-looking legs in the Caribbean."

She laughed. "It was the dream. I was wearing a ball gown and dreaming of an antebellum home. I was hurrying toward the house, toward something."

"Toward me," Christian said, and kissed her.

"Yes," she said. "Toward you." She touched his face. The worry she had seen in his eyes earlier had disappeared. She saw hope there now, and something she couldn't quite define, something she thought was love.

"Turn off the light," she said.

And when he did she came into his arms. "I think it would be nice..." She raised herself on one elbow so that she could look down at him. "I think it would be *very* nice if you made love to me."

"I'll have to think about it." He furrowed his brow and with a sigh said, "Oh, all right. If you insist."

She punched him and they both laughed. Then he kissed her and the laughter died.

Little by little the tensions of the day faded. They were one again, and it seemed to her in that moment when their bodies joined that together they could face whatever challenges tomorrow had to offer.

Chapter Thirteen

At nine the next morning Christian sat across the desk from President Philippe Bazaine. A dark-skinned man in his late sixties, Bazaine was in the middle of his eight-year term. Harvard educated, with leanings toward both the United States and France, he was, nevertheless, devoted to St. Dominique. In his first four years in office he had improved the roads, built two new schools, and had plans drawn up for rural clinics to be built in different parts of the island.

He knew, of course, all about the Dorset hotel chain and about the projected resort they wanted to build on his island. When Christian broached the subject he listened patiently for a few minutes, then interrupted to say, "I realize there are both good and bad points to the proposed project, Monsieur Dumond. For one side I hate to see a resort of the kind Dorset proposes to build mar our beautiful coastline. On the other hand I cannot help but think of the tourist business such a resort would bring and how that would help our economy."

He leaned back in his chair, hands folded over his stomach. "I want to build those rural clinics," he said. "And I want more schools. With the money Dorset's resort would bring in I'd have enough to build them."

"There are other sites on the island that are equally as good as the one Dorset wants," Christian said. "One is on the beach, the other is in the mountains. I believe if we stand firm and tell Dorset that particular piece of land is not for sale, they might very well accept one of the others."

"And if they don't?" Bazaine drummed a beat over his stomach. "If they don't, Monsieur Dumond, we will have lost a golden opportunity and a great deal of money."

Christian's jaw tightened. So much was at stake, he thought, perhaps even his job. But he had to try, he had to make the president see how much this meant to his people.

Speaking as calmly as he could, yet with great passion in his voice, Christian said, "I realize that, Monsieur le Président. But I believe we're talking about something more important than money."

"Is there such a thing?" Bazaine smiled.

"Yes, sir, there is. There's a responsibility to preserve our heritage." He looked directly into the president's eyes, his own eyes burning with the intensity of all that he was feeling. "Yours and mine, Monsieur le Président. We come from the same people, we are of the same blood. Our ancestors are buried on that land overlooking the sea. It belongs to them and to us and to the people who come after us because we are a part of them."

Christian's gaze did not waver, nor did Bazaine's. But it was Bazaine who looked away first. "There are men in my cabinet who want the resort," he said.

"Velmont and de Fossarieu."

The president nodded. "And others who wield a great deal of power. There are some, of course, who believe as you do. I myself . . ." He nodded. "I tend to agree with you, Monsieur Dumond. The land you speak of should be preserved, but frankly I don't see how I can oppose Velmont and de Fossarieu."

"If there were a law to protect the land . . ." Christian hitched forward in his chair. "There is such a law to preserve historic sites in the United States and I'm sure in other parts of the world. If we could pass such a law here, we could stop the monied interests who want the resort."

"And if there were such a law, Dorset would have no choice but to select a different site." President Bazaine swiveled his chair around and looked out of the window. "I want those clinics, but if there were a way . . ." For a moment or two he didn't speak, then he swiveled back around. "Perhaps we can have our cake and eat it, too, Monsieur Dumond. Wouldn't that be nice?"

"Wouldn't it, indeed." For the first time that morning Christian felt himself relax. "But a law takes time to pass," he said. "I'm not sure how much time we have."

"I am the President of St. Dominique, and as president I must admit I have occasionally done favors for friends and associates, as well as for members of my cabinet and parliament." He got up from behind his desk and came around to Christian. "It's time to call in some of those favors. I'll make a few phone calls and arrange some private meetings. There will be opposition but I can take care of it. As for Velmont and de Fossarieu..." Bazaine shrugged "...I've handled tougher men than them in my career."

Christian rose. "Thank you, Monsieur le Président."

"It may take a week, two at the most." Bazaine clapped a hand on Christian's shoulder. "I'm glad you came to see me, Monsieur Dumond. I needed to be reminded of who I am and what I stand for. Of what we both stand for." He looked thoughtful as he rubbed a hand across his jaw. "I have been looking ahead to the man who will take over when my term of office expires. I think today I have found that man."

"Monsieur le Président—"

"You have four years to think about it, Monsieur Dumond. And I have four years to persuade you." He walked with Christian toward the door. "Come to see me a week from today. If anything happens in the meantime, I will call you." He took Christian's hand. "I like you, Dumond. I like the man you are. I think that together we can pull this off. Don't give up hope that we will."

Don't give up hope. Christian wouldn't. He would hope and pray and believe that somehow, someway, the land would be saved.

Victor Reiger had tried to buy a suit in the hotel men's shop. The material was inferior and it would have taken a genius and ten days of hard labor to alter it enough to fit him. Instead, because he could not walk around the hotel with tomato juice all over his white suit, he bought a pair of pants and a shirt. The pants came three inches above his shoes and the shirt stretched tight across his back.

Furious, he had gone up to his room and sent for the bellman. "I want this suit cleaned by tomorrow morning," he'd said.

The bellman shook his head. "That is impossible, sir. This is Friday afternoon. The dry-cleaning establishment will not open until Monday morning. I could have it for you by Tuesday." He looked at the garment and shook his head. "With no guarantee that the stains can be removed."

Reiger clenched his jaw. Damn Laurel Merritt to eternal hell. He'd have her job if it was the last thing he ever did.

He had no choice but to cancel his appointment with Velmont and de Fossarieu. Velmont was angry but there wasn't anything Reiger could do; he couldn't go out dressed like he was. He called his wife and told her to send his blue suit by overnight express. Meantime he had no choice but to spend the weekend right here at the hotel.

He paced his room, then went out onto the balcony, his face taut with anger, hands clenched behind his back as he frowned down at the scene below. Then he focused on the bikini-clad bodies, young nubile women ripe for the picking, and a slow smile crossed his face. Maybe it wasn't going to be too bad a weekend after all.

As for Laurel... "I'll fix you," he said aloud. "Someway, someday, I'll fix you good."

Darcie Ann fluttered down the stairs of the plane; Virgie undulated.

"Darlin'!" Darcie Ann cried as she hugged Laurel. "Let me look at you. You're beautiful, baby, but oh, my, look at that tan. Shame on you, Laurel. You know what delicate skin we Merritt women have. You absolutely mustn't get in the sun, darlin'. It'll make you old and withered before your time."

Laurel took a deep breath. "I'm glad to see you, Mother. You look wonderful." She released her mother and turned to Virgie.

"Where's the Frenchman?" Virgie offered her cheek. "I thought he'd be with you."

"He had some things to do at the office. We'll see him later."

"I'm looking forward to it," Virgie drawled.

Laurel took another deep breath. "We're going to drive up in the mountains for dinner tonight," she said. "It's a nice place, I know you'll like it."

"I'd like just about any place with that cute ole Christian Dumond." Virgie linked her arm through Laurel's. "Aren't you the sly one. Getting him to invite you to stay with him the way you did."

"I'd been badly hurt, Virgie. Christian was kind enough to suggest I stay with him for a while."

"*Quite* a while." Virgie laughed. "You've always been such a stick, Laurel. Prim and proper as a church deacon. I reckon Christian must have something other men don't have. I've heard that Frenchmen are great lovers. It must be true." She winked. "I'd sure Lordy like to find out for myself."

"Virgie . . ." Laurel had vowed not to fight with her sister, but it took every bit of her willpower not to grab Virgie's shoulders and shake her senseless.

She drove her mother and sister to the hotel and went with them up to the penthouse suite Christian had reserved. There were flowers and fruit in the suite, and the view was spectacular.

"My, isn't this nice." Darcie Ann looked around. "But I'm still real sorry we couldn't stay with you, Laurel."

"Big sister doesn't want us around while she and Christian are making out."

"Virgie!" Darcie Ann glared at her younger daughter. "I absolutely will not stand for that kind of talk." She turned to Laurel. "You see? You see the kind of an example you're setting for your younger sister?"

Laurel gritted her teeth. Virgie had been sexually active since her fifteenth birthday, when she'd celebrated the occasion with Buford Lee Davis in the Davis family gazebo. She'd been married and divorced, and there hadn't been a time Laurel could remember when there wasn't a string of young men paying her court.

"You've been in St. Dominique for way over a month," Darcie Ann went on. "It was real nice of Christian to have you stay with him after the accident, but you should have come back to the hotel the minute you were feeling better. Instead you continued to live there, with him." She took a lace handkerchief from her purse and fanned her face with it. "I'm your mother. I have a right to know just what his intentions are."

"Mother—"

"Are you in love with him?"

"Yes."

"Well?"

"Well what?" Laurel asked, knowing exactly what her mother was after.

"Why hasn't he asked you to marry him?"

"There are things..." Laurel hesitated, then said, "There are things that have to be worked out."

"What things?"

"Christian's home is in St. Dominique, mine is in Georgia. And there's my job." Laurel shrugged. "There are things we need to talk about."

"Have you met his family?"

"Yes."

"I'd like to meet them."

Okay, Laurel told herself. Now's the time to tell her about Christian's mixed blood. And watch her swoon. She thought then of what her aunt Emily Rose had called "The Merritt family scandal." Her mother had never discussed with Laurel the fact that her husband had wanted to leave her for a black woman. It must have hurt and embarrassed her, especially back in the sixties, when racial barriers had been so strong in the South. Would that old wound, and the prejudice, come to the surface again when she found out that Christian was of mixed blood?

Hedging, Laurel said, "They live quite a way out of the city."

"If we're going to be here for a while, I don't see why we can't meet them. It's only proper that we do, seeing as how serious you and Christian seem to be about each other."

"Yes, well . . . perhaps we can arrange something." Laurel glanced at her watch. "I have to meet Christian at his office," she said. "Why don't the two of you rest for a little while? We'll pick you up a little after six."

"I'd certainly like to see where you live," Virgie said.

"Of course." Laurel picked up her purse. "We'll have cocktails at the house before we go to dinner." She kissed her mother's cheek. "I'm so glad you're here. I've missed you."

"And I've missed you, too, honey. We'll see you later, hear?"

"So Mama can have a heart-to-heart talk with your beau," Virgie offered.

Laurel clenched her fingers around her bag. "Six-thirty," she said, and headed for the door.

"Everything all right?" Christian asked when Laurel picked him up. "Your mother and sister get in on time?"

"Yes, and thank you for the fruit and flowers, Christian."

"Did they like the suite?"

"Yes, it's lovely." And because she didn't want to talk about her mother and Virgie, she said, "Did you see the president?"

Christian nodded.

"How did it go?"

"It went well, Laurel. Better than I expected. Bazaine has his heart set on building medical clinics in the more rural parts of the island and he needs money to do it, money that would come from the sale of land to Dorset. But I know now that he wasn't keen about selling the site over the sea. He listened to me when I suggested the preservation law. He liked the idea and he's going to do his best to get it passed. He figures that if Dorset wants a hotel here in St. Dominique they'll take one of the other sites." Christian reached for her hand. "Thanks to you, Laurel, this might work out after all."

"I'm glad, darling."

"You look tired."

"I am." She leaned against the seat and closed her eyes, and didn't open them until they reached the house.

They had a light lunch. They showered together, and then he said, "Why don't you rest for a while?"

"Alone?"

"Of course not." He put his arms around her and drew her close. "You need relaxing and I have just the prescription."

"What did you have in mind, Dr. Dumond?"

"An injection."

"Penicillin?"

He shook his head. "Vitamins C as in Christian and D as in Dumond."

Laurel smiled and for the first time that day felt some of her tension ease. She stepped out of his arms long enough to pull back the bedspread and the sheet.

In the time that followed she tried to put all of her thoughts and worries out of her mind, but she could not. When he asked, "What is it, Laurel? What's the matter?'' she kissed his shoulder and said, ''Nothing, Christian. I'm a little tired, that's all.''

He was gentle and loving, and infinitely patient. He touched her, caressed and kissed her until finally she began to respond. In that final moment she clung to him. ''I love you,'' she whispered. ''Always... always...''

And at last she slept.

He was gone when she awakened, but there was a note on his pillow that read, ''You were sleeping and I didn't want to wake you. I'm going to pick up your mother and sister.'' It was signed, ''With love, Dr. Dumond.''

Laurel smiled, then her smile faded. What would her mother say to him? She sighed, because there was very little she could do to silence her mother once Darcie Ann made up her mind that something needed to be said. Christian was a big boy and he could take care of himself. But she had visions of Darcie Ann saying, ''Darlin', when are you intending to make an honest woman out of my little girl?''

Laurel groaned and got up. She bathed again and dressed in an ankle-length, off-the-shoulder blue cotton dress, then brushed her hair off her face into a ponytail and fastened it with a cluster of gardenias. She had just put the finishing touches on her makeup when she heard Christian drive up.

''Off to the wars,'' she murmured, and with a final look at herself in the mirror she went out to meet her mother and Virgie.

They were out on the terrace. Christian had made planter's punches and Yveline had served hot hors d'oeuvres.

"This is just about the prettiest place I've ever seen." Darcie Ann smiled at Christian. "I can certainly see why Laurel isn't anxious to go back home. It's been real kind of you to take such good care of her, Christian, but I'm not sure I approve of her staying on here with you."

"Mother—"

"Now you just let me have my say, Laurel. I love you and I reckon I know what's best for you." She turned to Christian. "Laurel's daddy isn't here to take care of her so it's up to me to ask what your intentions are toward my little girl. I haven't said too much about her living here with you—"

"But you're going to now." Virgie drained her drink. "Could I have another one, darlin'?" She handed Christian her empty glass, and to her mother said, "You're embarrassing Christian, Mother. You really shouldn't, at least not until we've had dinner."

"I'm not embarrassed." Christian took Virgie's glass and filled it from the pitcher on the bar. "Laurel and I care a great deal for each other, Mrs. Merritt," he said. "When we decide what we're going to do you'll be the first to know. Until then..." he smiled "...why don't you just let us work things out for ourselves?"

"But I—"

"There's a beautiful place up the beach beyond those rocks that I'd like you to see. It's only a short walk and by the time we get back we'll be ready to leave for dinner. What do you say?"

Darcie Ann fluffed out her hair. "I can't think of anything I'd rather do," she murmured, and linked her arm through his.

"Smooth," Virgie said with a laugh when Christian led their mother away. "How come you and I have never learned to handle Mama that way?" She took a sip of her drink. "He's something else, big sister. I don't know how you managed to snag him, but I sure enough envy you. I bet he's dynamite in the sack."

"Virgie! For heaven's sake, Virgie!"

"Oh, come off it. We're both adults. Besides, I wasn't asking, I was only speculatin'." She leaned back in a chaise. "I met somebody today who knows you."

"Really? I know very few people in St. Dominique."

Virgie took a slow sip of her drink. "Victor Reiger," she said. "We met at the pool."

"Victor?" Laurel put her drink down. "He's bad news, Virgie. You shouldn't have anything to do with him."

"Why? Because the two of you have had a falling out? That hasn't anything to do with me. He asked me to dinner tomorrow night and I accepted."

"He's a married man."

"Well, darlin', he hasn't asked me for a lifetime commitment, only for dinner." Virgie took a sip of her drink. "I find him interesting in a brutish kind of way. Besides, this is my vacation and I plan on having some fun."

"Virgie—"

"I thought about asking Victor to join us tonight but I didn't. Wouldn't it have made for an interesting evening if I had?"

Laurel clenched her jaw and looked out toward the sea. There was nothing to do when Virgie was in this kind of a mood except to wait it out and hope for the best. She loved her mother and sister, but she wished with all her heart they had not come.

This was probably going to turn out to be the longest evening she had ever spent.

They went to the restaurant in the mountains where Christian had first taken Laurel.

Virgie had two martinis with her Oysters Rockefeller, white wine with her vichyssoise, and red with her steak. If there had been any way she could have arranged it, Laurel thought, she would have had Christian for dessert. Instead she settled for a cognac and coffee and a dance.

"I love island rhythms," she said, squirming up out of her chair. "Come and dance with me, Christian."

He looked across the table at Laurel. "Of course," he said.

She danced like Cynthia Jane Killigrew, her body pressed to his as she moved against him to the slowly seductive rhythm of the beguine. When she nuzzled his ear he held her away from him. "Behave yourself, little sister," he said.

"I'm Laurel's little sister." She laughed up at him. "Not yours."

"I'm very fond of her."

"Well, so am I, darlin'. Laurel's just about my most favorite person in the world, next to myself, of course. But when it comes to men..." She wrapped her arms around Christian to bring him closer. "When it comes to men," she said, "it's every sister for herself."

He thought the dance would never end, but when it finally did he led Virgie back to the table. All he could think about was getting this evening over with as quickly as he could, taking Laurel's mother and sister back to their hotel, and finally, please God, being alone with Laurel.

Virgie asked for another cognac. Darcie Ann said, "You've had enough, dear," and Virgie pretended she didn't hear.

"Well," Darcie Ann said to Christian. "Tell me all about your family. I'm just dying to meet them. What about your mother and father? Do you have brothers and sisters?"

"My parents are dead," he said. "I have two brothers and a sister. Jean-Luc lives in Paris, Michel in New York. My sister Solange and her little boy live with my grandmother."

"Is your grandmother from France?"

"No, she's an island woman."

"Of French descent, of course." Darcie Ann took a sip of her coffee. "I really know so little about St. Dominique, only that it's French and that it's just about the prettiest place I've ever seen." She smiled at Christian. "Tell me about your island," she said.

"What would you like to know?"

"Everything, especially about the French."

"They came to St. Dominique in the late 1600s. The Spanish had come much earlier, of course, but it was the French who really settled the island. They started in the sugarcane business, then began to import slaves from Africa."

"So much like our South." She smiled. "I just knew we had a lot in common."

Laurel held her breath. Christian looked at her and suddenly she knew what he was going to say next.

Don't, she wanted to tell him. Please don't do it. But she knew that he was going to.

"About eighty-five per cent of our people are descendants of the Carib Indians and African slaves," he told Darcie Ann. "So you see, most of the St. Dominicans, like me, are a combination of French, Indian, and African blood."

Coffee cup poised halfway between the table and her mouth, Darcie Ann stared at Christian.

"Oh, my God," Virgie said, and started to laugh.

"Do you...?" Coffee spilled over Darcie Ann's cup. "Do you mean...? Are you saying that you're...?" Her mouth moved but she couldn't get the word out.

"Part African? Why, yes," Christian said. "Didn't you know?"

"Did you...?" Wide-eyed, she turned to Laurel. "Did you know about this?"

"Yes, Mother." Laurel took Christian's hand, for though she was angry at him for having told her mother, she was even more angry at Virgie for laughing and for her mother's reaction. "Yes, of course I knew," she said.

Darcie Ann looked from one to the other of them. "This has to stop," she declared. "It can't go on!"

"What can't go on?" Christian asked.

"This... this whatever it is between you and Laurel."

"Love?" He tightened his hand around Laurel's. "We love each other, Mrs. Merritt. I'm not sure what the future holds for us, but for now it's enough to know how we feel about each other."

Laurel's mother looked at her, then at Christian. "I consider myself a reasonably sophisticated woman," she said. "But surely..." Her face tightened. "Surely you're not contemplatin' marriage."

"The subject of marriage hasn't come up, but when it does it will be a question that concerns only Laurel and myself."

"But you can't! What if you had children? They might be..." Darcie Ann picked up her napkin and dabbed at her lips. She turned to Laurel. "You couldn't," she said. "You just couldn't do that to me."

"Mother, please." Laurel took a deep breath and tried to ignore the sudden queasiness in her stomach. "Christian is right. This is between the two of us."

"But I'm your mother. Surely you have some family feeling, some sense of what is proper." She turned to Christian. "You don't understand," she said. "About my family, I mean. About our traditions."

"Lordy, Lordy," Virgie finished her cognac. "Wait'll I tell the folks back home."

Laurel pushed her chair back. "I'd like to leave," she said.

"But I haven't finished what I want to say," Darcie Ann protested.

"Yes, you have, Mother." Mad at everybody now, Laurel glared at Christian. "Are you ready?"

He put some bills on the table. "Ready," he said.

There was little conversation in the car. When they got to the hotel, both Christian and Laurel escorted her mother and Virgie to the door. When Laurel tried to kiss her mother's cheek, Darcie Ann turned away.

"We'll talk tomorrow," Laurel said.

Without answering, Darcie Ann turned and went into the hotel.

"Sorry," Virgie said. "I'm afraid you knocked the socks right off poor Mama. But I'm not my mama. I like a little spice in my life." She came closer and kissed Christian on the mouth.

He held her away from him. "Good night, Virgie," he said.

When they were back in the car and on their way to the beach house he turned to Laurel. "I had to tell them. They had to know."

She didn't answer.

"You're angry?"

"Not angry, but..." She looked out into the night.

"You didn't want me to tell them."

"Not like that."

He pulled the car to the side of the road and stopped. "Does it embarrass you that I'm of a mixed race?" he asked. "Are you ashamed that I am?"

"No, of course not. It's just..."

"Just what?"

She turned away from him. "I don't know," she said.

"I see." For a moment Christian didn't move, he simply stared ahead into the darkness. Then he started the car and they drove all the way to the beach house without speaking.

Chapter Fourteen

Laurel lay very still, and knew that Christian, too, could not sleep. Through the open but screened French doors she could hear the waves coming in hard against the shore, and the slap of palm fronds in the offshore breeze.

She knew that his thoughts were as troubled as hers. And that somehow tonight she had failed him.

He had asked her if she was embarrassed that he was of a different race, if she was ashamed of who he was. She remembered now that when she had met his grandmother he had asked her if it made a difference. She had not really answered him then, and she was not sure she had answered him tonight. She had never analyzed all that she felt for Christian, she had simply accepted the fact that she loved him.

The question of his mixed race had little to do with the man he was. She had seen his strength, she had experienced his tenderness. He was an exceptional man: the man she loved, the man she wanted.

She rested her hand on his naked thigh. When he didn't move or indicate that he was awake she began to caress him. He did not speak, but he reached to caress her, and they lay that way, touching each other, without speaking.

"My family hurt you tonight," she said at last. "I hurt you."

"No. It's all right. It doesn't matter."

"Yes, it matters."

"Your mother loves you. She wants what's best for you."

"You're best for me."

"Laurel—"

"Shh," she said and, rising up onto her elbow, she kissed him. "Tonight you told my mother that we love each other. You've never told me. You never said the words."

"They come hard for me. I was afraid to say them because I knew that when I did there would be no turning back."

"Say them."

"I love you," he said against her lips, and drew her down into his arms. But the tensions of the night were still with him. He had said the words she wanted to hear and he had meant them, but he knew they did not solve the problems he and Laurel still faced.

Laurel's mother and sister meant a great deal to her. Could she face their disapproval, their antipathy toward him, without it affecting what they meant to each other? What if they turned their backs on Laurel? What if in a real sense she could never go home again? Could her love survive if she were faced with the terrible burden, and yes, the guilt, of having gone against everything her mother believed in?

He had told her that he loved her, and he did. He loved her with a wholeness of heart and with a passion that knew no bounds. But there was fear with that love, and the terrible feeling that if she ever left him, he could not survive.

"Don't," she said, sensing his fear, and raised her body over his as though to shield him from worry, from doubt.

With a cry of need Christian tightened his arms around her. "I love you," he said again and again, making up for all the times he hadn't said the words. "I love you."

He rolled her beneath him. "Let me make love to you tonight, Laurel. Let me do all the things I want to do."

She caressed his shoulders, and gave herself up to the hands that touched her and to the lips that kissed her.

Every inch of her body came alive. Nerve endings caught fire, muscles quivered. She was completely his, malleable in his hands, surrendering herself with a wondrous gladness of heart.

And when at last he joined his body to hers she felt a depth of love, a oneness with another she had not thought possible. He was part of her, and she was part of him. Christian and Laurel together, joined in this sacred act of love.

In that final moment he took her cry and wrapped her in his arms. "Love," he said. "Oh, love."

And she felt his tears upon her cheeks.

Her mother phoned the following morning after Christian had left for his office.

"I'd like to see you," she said when Laurel answered. "Alone. Can you come to the hotel?"

"I don't have a car, Mother. I'll have to arrange for a driver."

"But you'll come?"

"Yes, of course."

"As soon as you can." Darcie Ann's voice wobbled. "I didn't sleep a wink last night. I just don't think I'll ever sleep again unless we get this straightened out."

"Yes, I agree that we need to talk. I'll be there as soon as I can."

She called Christian. "Do you think you could send a car for me?" she asked. "Mother called, she wants to see me."

"Of course. I should have thought of it this morning. I'll have a driver pick you up in an hour if that's soon enough."

It's too soon, she wanted to say, but didn't.

"Was your...?" Laurel heard him clear his throat. "Was your mother upset?" he asked.

"She sounded more tired than upset."

"I hate having you go through this. I'd offer to go with you but I'm afraid that would only make things worse."

"No, it's all right." Laurel tightened her hand around the phone. "Whatever happens between my mother and me, whatever she says . . . it won't change anything, Christian. I want you to know that."

"I do, Laurel. And I'll see you tonight. Would you like to go out?"

"No, darling. I'd rather stay here, just the two of us."

"The two of us," he said.

Darcie Ann was alone in the suite when Laurel arrived. "Virgie's down on the beach with that man from your office," she said. "I haven't met him, but Virgie says he's real nice." She looked at Laurel. "He's our own kind."

"Mother—"

Darcie Ann fluttered her manicured nails, stopping Laurel in midsentence. Dressed in a lacy pink peignoir that floated around her still-slender ankles, she coughed delicately, then settled into the chaise longue in front of the French doors that opened out onto the balcony.

Camille in her darkest moment, Laurel thought, then, overcome by guilt, said, "Aren't you feeling well, Mother?"

"I'll never feel well again if you don't come to your senses." She dabbed at her eyes. "I simply can't cope with this. I cannot believe that a daughter of mine actually thinks she's in love with a man of color."

"I don't think that I'm in love with Christian, Mother," Laurel said. "I *know* I am."

"And marriage? You can't actually be contemplating marriage."

"I am if he asks me."

"I'll die if you do. I'll flat-out die!"

Laurel took a steadying breath. "You liked Christian from the very first time you met him," she said in a reasonable tone. "You know you did."

"I thought he was French."

"He *is* French," Laurel said.

"With more'n a touch of the tar brush."

Laurel's mouth tightened. "I came because you asked me to," she said. "But I'm not going to stand here and let you say anything derogatory about Christian. Is that clear?"

Darcie Ann rolled her big blue eyes. "I can't understand it. You're just like your..." She shook her head, unable to go on, then reached for the glass beside her and to Laurel said, "Get my pills. They're on the nightstand next to my bed."

"What kind of pills?"

Darcie Ann closed her eyes and fanned herself with her handkerchief. "For my spells," she said.

"Spells?" Laurel asked as she headed into the bedroom.

"My nerves. The doctor says I have a delicate nature." She held out her hand when Laurel returned. "Give me two of them."

Laurel looked at the label on the bottle. "They're tranquilizers," she said.

"Well I *said* they were for my nerves."

"What are you drinking?"

"Just a little gin and tonic."

"Not with tranquilizers." Laurel put the two pills back in the bottle.

"What're you doing?" Darcie Ann sat bolt upright. "Those are my pills. You have no right—"

"I don't approve of tranquilizers," Laurel said. "But if you insist on taking them, then at least don't drink. Tranquilizers and alcohol don't mix."

"I need something to soothe my nerves." Darcie Ann took a sip of her drink. "It's all your fault that I'm feeling bad. Yours and that... that man's."

"His name is Christian."

"He ought to be ashamed of himself, trying to pass for white."

"He hasn't been trying to pass."

"Then why doesn't he tell everybody?"

"Tell everybody what? That's he's of mixed blood? Can you see him interrupting a conversation to say, 'Oh, by the way, I'm of Indian and African blood as well as French'?" Laurel shook her head. "I love Christian," she said. "Who he is is just fine with me."

"Have you thought about children?"

"Yes."

"Well? Do you intend having any if you marry?"

Laurel nodded. "I'd like two," she said. "More if it's all right with Christian."

"I'm appalled at your lack of good sense." Darcie Ann fluttered her handkerchief. "I can't believe that a daughter of mine, a daughter that I have worked and sacrificed for..."

Laurel tuned her out. She would stay for another five minutes and make whatever excuse she had to because she did not want to fight with her mother, nor did she want unkind words to pass between them. She would simply excuse herself and leave.

But before she could tell her mother that she was leaving, the door to the suite opened and Virgie came in. A black lace beach coat opened to reveal her bright red bikini. She had on red sandals, and her hair was in a pretty tangle down her back.

"Hi," she said to Laurel. "I've been down on the beach with that friend of yours."

"Victor Reiger?" Laurel frowned. "He's no friend of mine. I wish you'd stay away from him."

"Maybe I will after tonight. We have a dinner date."

"Virgie…" Laurel hesitated. "Look," she said, "I don't like to tell you what to do, but Victor Reiger has an edge to him that I don't like. He's crude and he's—"

Virgie laughed. "I'm a big girl, Laurel. I can take care of myself." She looked over at their mother. "Mama been telling you how shocked she is about that beau of yours?"

"Something like that," Laurel said.

"Well, you must admit that it was a bit of a surprise to find out we might have to welcome him into our family."

Darcie Ann whimpered, and with a wink Virgie said, "Come in the bedroom with me while I change, Laurel."

Once they were in her room, she laughed and said, "Poor Mama. She's scared to death the ladies of the Garden Club will find out about Christian. She'd never live it down if they did."

"What about you, Virgie? What's your position in this?"

"I think this whole thing's a hoot." She kicked off her sandals, shrugged out of the beach robe and dropped it on the floor. "Just don't bring home any little brown babies though. I don't reckon Mama could stand that."

"Dammit, Virgie—"

"Something I want to ask you." Virgie unsnapped the top of her bikini. "I've always heard that black men are..." she looked at herself in the mirror, cupped her breasts, and nodded with approval "...you know, bigger. I just wondered if Christian..."

Laurel didn't bother with a reply. She went out and slammed the door behind her.

They were on the beach, walking hand in hand, letting the warm sea water wash over their bare feet. Trade winds cooled the air, gulls floated motionless above them.

Christian knew she was unhappy. He wanted to help her but he didn't know how. Because he had experienced this kind of prejudice before, he knew exactly how difficult it was to handle. You could tell yourself that the people who shunned you because your skin was a different color than theirs, or because your eyes were slanted or you spoke with a strange accent did not matter. You could rationalize that their prejudice, whether inborn or acquired, was their problem, not yours. But it didn't help. Wherever and whenever there was prejudice there was gut-deep hurt.

Darcie Ann and Virgie were Laurel's family. She might disagree with them, she might fight with them, but it would hurt deeply if she were estranged from them. He didn't want that to happen.

Last night Laurel's mother had made it clear how she felt about such a relationship. Her family would never accept him. If he and Laurel were to marry...

He tightened his hand around hers. He wanted to marry Laurel. He wanted to have children with her. But would that be fair to her?

He thought of how it had been last night, of how they had loved each other. And knew that never again would he find with a woman what he had found with Laurel. He loved her, and he would keep on loving her until the day he died.

"I know how difficult this is for you," he said. "I know how torn you are about all of this, about your mother and your sister, and about what you feel for me."

Laurel stopped and faced him. "I'm not torn in the way I feel about you, Christian. I love you. I want to spend the rest of my life with you."

"As I do with you." He took her hands in his. "But we have to face the fact that there are differences, Laurel, very real problems of race and of culture. And there is your family to consider."

She shook her head. "I won't let my family come between us."

"They're your family. I know you love them."

"And I love you," she said, desperation creeping into her voice. "Oh, Christian, I love you so."

"Laurel . . ." He felt as though his body were being torn in two. "We need to give this a little time," he said.

She looked at him, her expression guarded, her body gone suddenly still. "What . . . what do you mean?" she asked.

He took a steadying breath. "I think you should go back to Atlanta for a while. We need time to think this through."

"I don't need time!"

Christian let go of her hands. "But I do," he said.

She looked at him, unbelieving. She saw the truth in his eyes. Turning away, she said, "I'll leave to-night. I'll go to the hotel."

"No." He gripped her shoulders and brought her around to face him. "I don't mean to hurt you," he said. "I love you."

She began to weep. "Then why...?" She shook her head. "I don't understand," she said.

"If we're going to have a life together, we have to be sure, Laurel." He put a finger under her chin and lifted her face to his. "If we marry, it will be for a lifetime. I'll never let you go."

"But you're letting me go now."

"Only until you're sure. You need to go home, back to your own life, your own country."

She wanted to plead with him, to get down on her knees and beg him to let her stay. But she could not. If he wanted her to leave, she would leave. And it came to her then that he wasn't sending her away only so that she could think things through, but to give him-self time. For if they were to marry, he, too, would be making a change in his life.

A feeling of utter hopelessness washed over Laurel. She loved Christian; she did not doubt his love for her. But perhaps he was right, perhaps there were too many problems for them ever to make a go of it.

She turned away from him and they started back the way they had come. He reached for her hand and she gave it to him. But they did not speak. They looked for a moment at the sunset, those glorious colors of red and flamingo, of burnt orange and gold, then away as though they could not bear to look upon such beauty when their world was crashing in upon them.

He saw her tears, but didn't say anything. He only held her hand until they reached the house.

The call came a little after three that morning. Christian, more asleep than awake, reached for the phone. He listened for a moment, then said, "What? What happened? Yes, she's here. Just a moment."

He turned on the bedside light. "It's your mother," he said, touching Laurel's shoulder.

"Mother?" Laurel sat up and rubbed her eyes.

He handed the phone to her and she said, "Mother? What is it? Is something wrong?"

"Laurel! Laurel, you've got to come! I can't handle this. I can't—"

"What is it? Are you ill? What—?"

"It's Virgie!"

"Virgie? What do you mean? Is she all right?"

"No!" Darcie Ann was weeping, hysterical. "That man!" she cried. "That terrible man!"

"What man?" Laurel looked at Christian. "Try to calm down, Mother. Who are you talking about?"

"That man from your office."

"Victor Reiger?"

"He hit her, and he...he... Oh, God, Laurel, you've got to come."

Laurel held the phone against her breast. "Reiger," she told Christian. "He's hurt Virgie. He—"

He took the phone from her. "Where is Virgie now, Mrs. Merritt?" he asked.

"Here," Darcie Ann managed to say. "I want her to go to a hospital but she won't go." She began to sob. "I don't know what to do," she wailed.

"Do what you can for Virgie, Mrs. Merritt," Christian said. "Laurel and I will be there in twenty minutes."

He put the phone down. Laurel was already pulling on a pair of jeans. Her face was white, her hands were shaking. "It's my fault," she said. "I should have stopped her from going out with Reiger. Oh, damn him! If he's hurt her because of me, I'll—"

"Stop it!" Christian said. "This isn't your fault. If Reiger hurt her, it's because he's a brute and a bastard, not because of you."

Laurel took a deep breath. "Okay," she said. "Okay."

"I'm going to call a doctor I know," Christian said. "Just in case."

Laurel clenched her hands together and tried to stop shaking. "Yes," she said. "Just in case."

He made the call. "We'll meet you at the hotel," he said. Then he dressed quickly, and taking Laurel's arm, he hurried with her to the car. They spoke little on the way to the hotel. All that Laurel could think about was how Virgie had looked earlier today in her bright red bikini, and how she had lifted her breasts to admire herself in the mirror. And that Victor Reiger had hurt her and that she wanted to kill him.

She opened the window and drew in great gulps of the fresh sea air.

Christian covered her hand with his. "Take it easy," he said.

He drove fast, but carefully, and fifteen minutes after they had left the house he pulled up in front of the hotel. They hurried in and up to the suite. He knocked and Darcie Ann, her face ravaged with tears, opened the door.

"Oh, Lord," she said, and flung herself into Laurel's arms.

Laurel hugged her, then held her away. "Where's Virgie?" she asked.

Darcie Ann gestured toward the bedroom. "I don't know what to do," she wailed. "I just don't know what to do."

"Stay here with Mother," Laurel said to Christian. "I'm going in to Virgie."

She knocked at the door, then opened it. Virgie lay on her side away from her, curled into a fetal position, one hand hiding her face.

"Virgie?" Laurel sat beside her. "I'm here, dear. It's going to be all right now." She brushed her sister's tangled hair back from her face.

Virgie looked up at her. One eye was swollen shut. A purple bruise marred her cheek and her lip was cut. Laurel sucked her breath in. It took every ounce of her will not to cry out.

"Tell me what happened," she said as calmly as she could.

"We had dinner here and . . . and then we went for a walk on the beach and we . . . we kissed a few times. That's all. He . . . he wanted me to go up to his room for a nightcap." She gulped. "You know me," she whispered. "Anything for a laugh."

"I know."

"I knew he probably wanted to go to bed with me. I didn't feel that way about him but I...I figured that I could handle it." She reached for Laurel's hand. "I always have before. I mean, if I didn't want to, I could always talk myself out of it. But Victor..." Virgie shuddered. "He's so mean, Laurel. He just...just pushed me down on the bed and started ripping my clothes. I...I tried to get away from him and he said I'd been teasing him long enough. I slapped him and he..." Virgie turned away. "He was so strong. I couldn't get away from him and he...he raped me, Laurel."

Laurel put her arms around her sister and drew her close. "It's all right, baby," she said. "It's all right. I'm with you now, Virgie."

There was a knock on the door and Christian called out, "Laurel? The doctor is here. May we come in?"

"Just a minute." She held Virgie away from her. "Christian's brought a doctor, dear," she said. "Let's let him have a look at you."

"But I don't want—"

"Please, Virgie. It's important that you do."

Virgie took a shaking breath. "All right," she murmured.

"Come in, Christian," Laurel said.

He came in. "This is Doctor Verneuil," he said.

"*Madame.*" The doctor offered his hand to Laurel. "This is your sister?"

"Yes." She hesitated. "Virgie...?"

Virgie stared at the doctor. "You're black," she said.

He held one hand out in front of him. "Good Lord! You're right." He smiled. "Would it make you feel better if I tell you I graduated from the University of Michigan Medical School and that I did my residency at Johns Hopkins?"

A reluctant smile crept into the corners of Virgie's mouth. "I reckon it would," she said.

"I need to examine you," he told her. "I think you'd feel more comfortable with your sister in the room."

Virgie looked at Laurel. "You'll stay?" she asked.

"Of course," Laurel said, and took her sister's hand.

Dr. Verneuil was thorough. He cleaned the cut on Virgie's lip and touched the skin around her swollen eye. He draped her with a sheet. His touch was careful, gentle.

"I'm going to give you something to help you sleep tonight," he said when he finished the examination. "And these pills for any discomfort you might have. I'll be back in the morning to check on you."

"Thank you, Doctor. You've been ..." Virgie hesitated. "You've been real nice," she said.

He touched her shoulder. "Try to rest now, *mademoiselle.*" He turned to Laurel. "Perhaps you could stay with her tonight?" he asked.

"Yes, I'll stay." Laurel kissed her sister's forehead. "I'll be back in just a few minutes," she assured her sister.

When she and the doctor went into the other room Christian was on the phone.

"I see," he said. "Thank you." He put the phone down. "Reiger checked out an hour ago." He looked at his watch. "He'll be at the airport, the first flight out is at seven." He started toward the door.

"Christian, don't! Victor's a powerful man. He—"

"And I'm an island man." He nodded to the doctor. "We appreciate your coming," he said. "Will Virgie be all right?"

"Physically, yes. But rape is an ugly thing, Christian. It will take her time to recover from the psychological effect."

"I see." Christian put his arm around Laurel. "Your mother is in the bedroom. I assume you'll want to spend the night."

"Yes, I told Virgie I would." She looked up at him. "I wish you wouldn't go after Victor," she said.

Christian kissed the top of Laurel's head, but he didn't answer. He held out his hand to Dr. Verneuil. "Thank you for coming," he said. "We appreciate it."

"We're friends," Verneuil said. "Of course I would come." He turned to Laurel. "Your sister is a beautiful young woman. Let us hope that Christian will bring the word of the gospel to Mr. Reiger and make a true believer out of him."

"I intend to." Christian squeezed Laurel's shoulder. "I'll talk to you in the morning," he said.

The two men left together. When she was alone Laurel went to the phone and asked the operator to connect her with a number in Atlanta.

The phone rang six times before Eli picked it up. "Whoziss?" he said in a voice muffled with sleep.

"Laurel Merritt."

"Laurel? What...? What in the hell? It's four-thirty in the morning here."

"It's four-thirty in the morning here, too."

"Are you out of your mind, calling me at this hour?"

"No, Eli, I'm not out of my mind. But I'm very, very angry."

"Now see here," he said. "You can't call—"

"Shut up," she said. "About an hour ago Victor Reiger raped my sister. He's probably at the airport now waiting for a plane. If Christian doesn't kill him, Victor will be on the seven o'clock plane. If you don't agree right now to fire him, I'm going to call the local police and have him arrested. Then I'm going to call the Atlanta papers. I prefer not to cause a scandal because of my sister, but I will if I have to. Do you understand me, Eli?"

"Are you sure? Of what happened, I mean?"

"Damn sure! A doctor has examined Virgie. I have no doubt at all that he will sign a statement certifying that Virgie has been raped and brutalized." Laurel clutched the phone. "Well? Do I have your word that you'll fire him or do I contact the police and the newspapers?"

"I don't want a scandal."

"I didn't think you did." She tightened her hand around the phone. "Another thing, Eli. You'll also see to it that Victor never works in the state of Georgia again."

"You're pushing it."

"You bet I am. Well?"

"Okay!" he shouted. "I'll see that he's black-balled from every chain of hotels from here to Istanbul."

"Thank you."

"You're welcome." Eli hesitated. "When are you coming back?"

"As soon as Virgie's able to travel."

"We'll talk when you do."

"Sure, Eli." She put the phone down. Her hands were shaking but she felt a lot better than when she'd first walked into Virgie's room.

She went then to check on her mother. Darcie Ann was in bed. Her eyes were swollen from weeping.

"Has the doctor gone?" she asked.

"Yes, Mother."

"He's black."

"I know." Laurel patted her mother's shoulder. "I'm going to spend the night with Virgie," she said. "You rest now."

"All right." Darcie Ann's lips trembled. "You're a good daughter, Laurel. I don't know what we'd do without you."

"Or I without you."

She went out and closed the door, and went into Virgie's bedroom.

"Come into bed with me," Virgie said in a trembly voice. "Like we used to when we were little and you took care of me."

Laurel took her shoes off. She lay down beside Virgie and put her arms around her.

"I hurt, Laurlie," Virgie whispered, calling Laurel by the childhood name neither of them had thought of in years. "Sing me a song like Papa used to."

And Laurel sang:

"Hush little baby, don't you cry,
Daddy's gonna sing you a lullaby..."

"Go to sleep, Virgie," she said. "Go to sleep, little sister."

Chapter Fifteen

A week had passed. Virgie was better, but her right eye was still swollen and the bruise on her cheek had faded to an ugly yellow. She was quiet and withdrawn, spoke when she was spoken to, but other than that had little to say.

During their adult years the two sisters had grown apart. Laurel had not approved of Virgie's life-style and very likely Virgie had not approved of hers. But what had happened had brought them close again, and often in the evening they would sit together out on the balcony overlooking the sea.

On one such evening Virgie said, "I've said hateful things about Christian and I'm sorry. Maybe I said them because I'm jealous of you, jealous that a man as fine and good as Christian loves you."

Laurel looked out toward the sea. "Yes," she said. "He loves me." She swallowed hard. "He thinks we should give it more time, Virgie. He wants me to go back to Atlanta."

"Don't go."

"I'm afraid I have to. And maybe Christian is right, maybe we do need more time." She turned to Virgie. "Both Christian and I have to want this," she said. "Unless we do, unless both of us are sure of how we feel, it isn't any good."

"But you love him."

"Oh, yes. I love him."

"Then fight for him."

"I don't know how," Laurel said.

And it was true, she didn't. Christian had said he wanted her to go home to think things through, but somehow she knew that she wasn't the one who needed time to think. He was the one who was uncertain, he was the one who needed time.

It was decided, because her mother and sister needed her, that she would return to Atlanta with them at the end of the week.

Christian saw her only at breakfast and in the evening when he picked her up from the hotel. It was, it seemed to Laurel, as though they were rehearsing for the separation to come, as though little by little they had begun to accept the fact that soon they would be parted.

He had returned to the hotel the afternoon after Reiger's attack on Virgie. Laurel had looked at his skinned knuckles but she hadn't asked him any questions. Nor did he tell her what had happened.

He had found Reiger at the airport bar. Reiger's face had borne scratch marks. He'd been defensive and belligerent.

"Rape?" he'd said when Christian, having suggested they step outside, confronted him. "Are you kidding? The dame was asking for it. She and that sister of hers think they're better than anybody else. Next time it'll be her sister I—"

That was when Christian had hit Reiger. The fight had been hard and vicious. The last time Reiger went down, Christian picked him up, dusted him off, and toe-walked him into the first-aid station.

He had told Reiger when he helped him board that if he ever came near Laurel or Virgie again, he would kill him.

"Don't try to see them or phone them," he'd said. "If I ever hear that you have, I'll hunt you down." Then he'd eased Reiger into his seat. "Have a nice flight," he said.

They were having breakfast on the terrace overlooking the sea on the day before Laurel would fly back to Atlanta with her mother and sister.

They had been very quiet with each other these last few days. As though suffering a bereavement, they spoke softly and touched each other gently, for in a way neither of them could explain they had already parted and the time for grieving was upon them. Their few attempts at conversation dwindled and died. When they spoke it was about her mother and sister, not about themselves.

Laurel said, "I'd like to drive out to Le Carbet today and say goodbye to your grandmother and Solange. And I have a goodbye present for Etienne."

Goodbye. Such a final-sounding word. Christian looked at her, then away. "Of course," he said. "We can leave right after breakfast."

Time was running out. There were so many things he wanted to say, but the words would not come. Last night they had made love, slowly, tenderly, and in that final moment his only thought had been, one more day, one more night.

There were clouds hanging low over the sea and the threat of a storm was in the air when they left for Le Carbet. Christian asked if she wanted the top up on the car and she said, "No, leave it down. The smell of the sea is different today."

"A storm is coming. The fishing boats are heading in toward shore."

"Maybe it will blow over."

Christian shook his head. "The fishermen know," he said.

There was a mist in the mountains. Heavy and wet, it shrouded the trees and enveloped the car, closing them into a silence of unreality.

Laurel rested her hand on his leg and he said, "Don't be afraid. We'll be out of this soon."

"I'm not afraid." She studied his face through the mist that covered, wanting to say, I wish we could stay here forever, cut off from everything and everybody, just the two of us here in the cool gray mist.

In a little while they started down toward Le Carbet. Christian had phoned ahead and his grandmother and sister and Etienne were waiting for them when they arrived.

"We're going to have lunch in the dining room because the weather is not so nice today," Maria said after she greeted them. "If the storm comes, then you will spend the night."

"I'm afraid I can't," Laurel said. "I'm leaving St. Dominique tomorrow."

"You're leaving? But why? I thought that you..." Marie looked at Christian, then back to Laurel. "I thought you were going to stay."

"My sister..." Laurel hesitated. And because she did not want to tell Marie the truth about what had happened to Virgie, said, "My sister hasn't felt well since she's been here. It would be best if I returned to Atlanta with her and my mother to make sure they make the trip all right."

"But you will come back, of course."

"I'm not sure when, *madame*. I've been away from my job for a long time. I have to get back to it."

Marie looked at Christian. He dropped his gaze.

"You going away?" Etienne's lower lip came out in a pout. "We never went fishing," he said.

"Fishing?" Laurel looked thoughtful. "That reminds me. I do believe there's something in the car for you."

"For me?"

"I'm pretty sure there is. Why don't you and I go have a look."

He took her hand and almost pulled her out the door.

"That's one fine lady," Solange said with a smile. "How come you're letting her get away from you?"

"How come you don't fix me a nice tall planter's punch?" Christian said.

"And stop asking questions?" Solange grinned. "Planter's punches coming up, big brother."

"I will ask the same question," Marie said when Solange left the room. "But I expect an answer."

"*Grandmère*..." Christian hesitated. "It's true about Laurel's sister. She hasn't been well. Dr. Verneuil has seen her several times. She'll be more comfortable if Laurel makes the flight back to Atlanta with her."

"But it's more than that, isn't it?"

Christian turned away and went to stand by the windows that looked out onto the gardens. "Laurel and I come from different backgrounds, *Grandmère*. We—"

"Does she love you?"

"Yes."

"Then why does she want to leave you?"

"She doesn't. I'm the one who thinks she should go, at least for a while. We need to give each other time to think things through."

"Rubbish! Either you love each other or you don't."

"Laurel and I are different," he said.

"As different as your grandfather and I were?" Marie got up and went toward him. "I cannot tell you what to do but I wish I could. I can only tell you that if the love is true, you are wrong to let it go. You..." She reached out for him. "Oh," she said. "I..." She swayed and would have fallen if he hadn't put his arms around her.

"What is it?" he asked, alarmed.

"Just . . . just a bit of dizziness. I'll be all right in a moment."

He led her to a chair and knelt beside it. "What can I get you? Do you have medicine? Shall I get it?"

"No, no. It's nothing, really." She leaned her head back against the chair and closed her eyes.

Christian took her hand. Until this moment he had not realized how much his grandmother had aged in the last few months. There were lines on her face he had not seen before, bruiselike patches of darkness under her eyes.

He began to stroke her forehead and she said, "Pierre used to do that. He has been so much in my thoughts these past few days, Christian. He comes to me in my dreams, as young and handsome as he was when first we met. And I am beautiful again." She opened her eyes. "Love never dies," she said. "Neither time nor age nor death can diminish it." She rested her hand on the top of his head. "If we are lucky enough to find it, we are truly blessed."

"Grandmère—"

"What is it?" Solange called from the doorway. Alarmed, she hurried to her grandmother's side.

"It's nothing," Marie said. "A momentary dizzy spell. I'm quite all right now."

"I think it would be a good idea if you came back to Port-au-Mer with Laurel and me tonight," Christian said. "I'd feel better if we let Dr. Verneuil take a look at you."

"And I'll feel better right here in my own home." Marie patted Christian's hand. "Now bring me my drink and stop fussing."

He looked at Solange. She shrugged and said, "I've been trying to get her to see a doctor for weeks but she won't budge. And she still insists on working with her orchids every day."

"My orchids give me pleasure," Marie said. "Now stop fussing and help me up."

Laurel and Etienne returned, he with a brand-new rod and reel, and so excited he couldn't stand still.

"Look what Laurel gave me!" he exclaimed.

"It's beautiful." Solange looked at Laurel. "That was nice of you," she said. "Thank you."

"It was my pleasure." Laurel rested a hand on Etienne's shoulder. "I'm going to miss him," she said.

"He'll miss you, too. When you come back you must stay with us, Laurel. We would love to have you here."

"And we can go fishing." Etienne beamed a smile up at Laurel. *"Oui?"*

"Oui," she answered.

If she came back. She tried not to think about that.

The day darkened. Christian went out to put the top up on his car. They had a pleasant lunch but by the time they had finished, rain began to spatter. In the distance they heard the roll of thunder and a flash of lightning split through the heavy dark clouds.

"We'd better be starting back," Christian said. "I want to get through the mountains before it gets any worse."

"A few more minutes," Marie said. "I want to show Laurel a new orchid." She stood, steadying herself for a moment or two at the back of her chair before she took Laurel's hand. "Come along, my dear. I have a real beauty that I want you to see."

It was a beauty, pure white with a deep purple throat touched with yellow. Laurel looked at it, unable for a moment to speak. Then said, "Oh, *madame,* it's truly the most beautiful flower I have ever seen."

"I want you to have it."

"No, I couldn't."

But it was too late. Marie had already cut it. And handing it to Laurel, she said, "It's as beautiful as you are, my dear." Then she kissed Laurel. "Return to us," she whispered. "Return to Christian."

Laurel put her arms around Marie Dumond. Unable to speak, her emotions close to the surface, she could only murmur, "I will, *madame.* Someday I will."

The rain had worsened by the time they returned to the house. Christian said, "We really must leave now, Laurel."

But she was reluctant to say goodbye. She wanted to stay here with him, with his grandmother and Solange and little Etienne.

Solange hugged her, and so did Etienne. Marie clasped her shoulders. "Come back to us," she whispered when Laurel kissed her cheek.

Then Christian took Laurel's hand and they hurried out to the car.

Rain beat against the windows, so hard it was difficult to see. The wind rose and the branches from overhanging trees broke and slapped against the windshield. When the windows clouded he put the air-conditioning on high, then the defroster. Their headlights beamed through heavy fog, ghostly beacons in the night. They didn't speak. He drove with both hands gripping the wheel, taking the mountain curves slowly, carefully. Laurel switched the radio on, found only static, and finally the music of the beguine. It made her think of the day in Saint Esprit when they had danced in the village square.

When they started down from the mountain the fog lifted and below they could see the lights of Port-au-Mer.

"We're almost home," Christian said.

Your home, she thought. Not mine.

It was not until they reached the house and went in through the rain that she saw that the white orchid had died.

"Oh, no." She stared at it, unbelieving. "It was so beautiful," she said. "I wanted to keep it because your grandmother had given it to me."

"I'm sorry," Christian said. "It was the air-conditioning. I'm sorry."

Laurel didn't answer. She only looked at the orchid, and could not hold back the tears that rose and fell.

"It's a real good day to fly," Darcie Ann said.

"Yes." Laurel looked at Christian, then away.

They'd had little to say to each other this morning. The night before they had made love, he with urgent desperation, she with a sadness she could not disguise. Afterward they had held each other without speaking, for there was little to say.

They picked up her mother and Virgie at the hotel. Darcie Ann, always a nervous flier, chattered. Virgie, who wore big dark sunglasses to disguise her swollen eye, was silent.

Christian helped them check their bags. "The skies are clear all the way to Miami," he told them. "You'll have a smooth flight."

"Thank the Lord," Darcie Ann said.

After that it seemed as though there was nothing to say. Laurel wished they'd call the flight so that this could be over with, but when they did she was overcome by a feeling of panic. It was too soon. She couldn't leave him yet. She didn't want to go.

"There's Doctor Verneuil," Christian said.

He came toward them through the crowd waiting for the plane to be called. *"Mon Dieu,"* he exclaimed. "I was afraid I wouldn't get here in time." He handed Virgie a bouquet of pink roses. "For you, Mademoiselle Virginia," he said. "I hope that you have a safe and happy trip and that you will return soon.'

Virgie opened her mouth, closed it, then managed to say, "Thank you, Doctor Verneuil."

"My name is Jacques," he said.

"Oh." Virgie cleared her throat. "It was kind of you to come to the airport." Then, taking a deep breath, she said, "If you ever come to Atlanta, please call me. Christian will know the number."

"I will indeed, *mademoiselle.*"

There was another announcement over the loudspeaker, first in French, then in English.

"That's your flight." Christian held out his hand. "Goodbye, Mrs. Merritt," he said. "Goodbye, Virgie."

"Goodbye, Christian." Virgie put her arms around him. "Thank you for everything. I'm sorry I was such trouble for you."

He managed a smile. "Come back when you can," he said. "You're always welcome."

She let him go and offered her hand to Dr. Verneuil. Instead of shaking her hand he kissed it. She smiled and with just a touch of her old flirtatious self said, "*Adieu,* Doctor. Perhaps we'll see each other again."

"I will live in hope," he answered.

"We'd better board," she said to her mother.

"Yes, it's time." Christian rested his hands on Laurel's shoulders. "I'll call you tonight, *ma chère.*"

She nodded, unable to speak.

"I'll miss you."

"I..." She couldn't go on.

He drew her into his arms. "Goodbye, my dear," he whispered against her cheek. "Take care."

"You, too." She wanted to say something else, wanted to say so many things. But the words wouldn't come.

He kissed her and said, "I love you," against her lips.

"Love..." she whispered, her throat working with the effort not to cry.

"I know," he said.

"Laurel darlin'! If you don't come on we're going to miss the plane."

He let her go. Virgie put her arm around her and together the two sisters followed their mother onto the jetway, and out of sight.

"Would you like a drink?" Jacques Verneuil asked.

Christian took a shaking breath. "Yes," he said. "A drink." And knew it wouldn't help.

Chapter Sixteen

Two weeks after Laurel returned to Atlanta a law was passed by the St. Dominican parliament declaring that the burial ground overlooking the Caribbean was sacred land and that it, as well as the surrounding area, would henceforth be declared a historic site and would be preserved as such.

A week later Hal Ginsburg, Dorset's chief architect, arrived in St. Dominique. Christian showed him the two pieces of land he had shown Laurel. Ginsburg thought the one on the beach would do but when he saw the place in the mountains that had so impressed Laurel he said, "Yes, this is it."

A price was agreed on; the deal was made. That night the two men celebrated with a bottle of champagne and dinner at one of Port-au-Mer's finest beachfront restaurants.

Ginsburg, a small olive-skinned man with an aesthetic face and dark brown eyes, touched his glass to Christian's. "Done and done," he said. "Shall we drink to it and to Miss Merritt? She's the one who talked Dorset into sending me here when the other land was declared a national monument." He smiled. "Eli ranted and raved, mostly at Laurel, when he heard about it. But she stood up to him and finally he gave in and agreed to let me have a look at the other two properties." He took a sip of his champagne. "She's quite a woman, Mr. Dumond."

"Yes," Christian said. "She's quite a woman."

The days since Laurel had left passed slowly and painfully. Each morning he had a lonely breakfast, served on the terrace by a silent Yveline.

The morning after Laurel's departure, Yveline asked, "When the Mademoiselle Laurel be coming back?"

And when Christian answered, "I don't know," she had glared at him as though he had done some terrible deed.

Perhaps he had. Perhaps he shouldn't have sent Laurel away. He had done what he thought was best for both of them, but as the days passed he wondered if, after all, it had been the right thing to do. "Love is simple," his grandmother had told him. And Laurel had said, "To turn your back on love would be like laughing in the face of the gods. Like saying, 'Take back your gift. I have no need of it.'"

Is that what he had done? By sending Laurel away had he laughed in the face of the gods?

The day his government signed the land deal with Dorset he called her.

"Thanks to you it's all going to work out," he said.

"I'm so glad." He heard the hesitation in her voice. "How are you, Christian?"

"Fine," he said too heartily. "Just fine."

"And your grandmother? How is she?"

"She hasn't been too well, Laurel. I brought her to Port-au-Mer to see Dr. Verneuil last week."

"What's the matter? Is she all right now?"

"She's better."

"What did Dr. Verneuil say?"

"That she has to slow down. But that's difficult for her. She's been active all her life. I'm afraid . . ." And because he did not want to give voice to his fears, he said, "I'm afraid we'll have a difficult time holding her down."

"You'll let me know how she is?"

"I will."

He heard her other phone ring. "I've got to go," she said. "Give my love to your family."

"Yes, of course." He hesitated. "Laurel . . ."

"I've really got to go. I . . ." He heard her voice break. "Good . . . goodbye, Christian."

He rested his hand on the phone for a moment or two after she hung up, as though by that tenuous thread he could still hear her voice. She'd rung off so abruptly, as though in a hurry to cut him off, to be finished with the only communication they had.

He had sent her away to give her time to think. Had she changed her mind about the way she felt about him? Panic tightened his chest. Call her back, he told himself. Tell her all the things you want to tell her. Tell her to come back to you.

But still he sat, his hand on the phone. And did not make the call that would return her to him.

Laurel threw herself into her job. She was at the office at eight and often stayed until after seven every evening, reluctant to return to her silent apartment and a frozen dinner in front of the television set.

On the weekends she went home, partly because she was restless, partly because she knew Virgie needed her.

Her sister was more subdued. She had lost her Southern belle flirtatiousness that had been known to charm and captivate every male on the southern side of the Mason-Dixon line. She refused dates, and when Darcie Ann, all in a flutter, told Virgie that Boone Lockwood was back from Birmingham and that he'd told her his marriage had been a terrible mistake and that he couldn't wait to see Virgie, Virgie had frowned and said, "Don't be silly, Mother."

"You need to go out," Laurel told her. "Not necessarily with Boone, but it's time you started accepting dates."

Virgie shook her head. "I'm not ready to start that merry-go-round again," she said. "I may never be ready."

Summer faded into fall. The leaves of the sweetgum tree turned to a brilliance of gold and darkening green, the sassafras to rich orange and red. The air was soft, with just the barest hint of morning and evening chill.

One early Sunday morning before her mother and sister were up, Laurel put on a sweater over her shoulders and went to walk in the wooded lane in back of the house. Almost two months had passed since she had left St. Dominique. The last time Christian had called, their conversation had been stilted. Like polite strangers they had talked about the weather, her job and his job. They'd started clearing the land, he told her. Hal Ginsburg was working on the architectural layout, she told him.

"I'll call again," he said just before he hung up. "Take care."

"You, too."

Now as she walked along the dusty path that led into the more densely wooded area, she wondered how it came about that two people who had been so close, who had shared that most intimate of human passion, could grow apart. She loved Christian Dumond to the very depths of her soul, but she could not forever wait and hope that someday he would change his mind.

A few days before, Eli had told her that Dorset was building a new hotel in the Loire Valley. If she wanted to go to France, he would arrange it.

She thought that she would. She needed to get away. It would improve her French.

French. Remembered words whispered in the dark echoed in her mind. Words of passion and of love....
"Ma très chère. Je t'aime tant."

Laurel looked about her at the loveliness of autumn and her heart cried out, Christian. Christian.

It was after nine by the time she cut through the trees and started back toward the house. Dry leaves crunched underfoot and the woods came alive with birdsong. She would miss this place, and her mother and her sister. But it was time to get on with her life.

She paused at the edge of the trees and looked toward the house where she had grown up. She loved this land, this rich red Georgia clay that was a part of her. But she would have given it up, she would have walked away without ever looking back if Christian had asked her to. But he hadn't. She did not think she would ever forgive him for that.

As she came closer she saw that there was a car parked in the driveway with a rental sticker on the back bumper. Boone, she thought. And wondered what Virgie would say to him.

She came up the front drive. The door opened and a man came out. The sun was in her eyes and she could only make out the dark shape of him. If it was Boone, she was going to have a talk with him. He couldn't hurt Virgie the way he had.... She stopped. It wasn't Boone. This man was taller.

He lifted his arm, then he came down the steps and started toward her. "Laurel!" he called out. "Laurel!"

She began to run toward him, as he ran toward her, then she was in his arms, holding him as he held her, crying his name, "Christian, Christian," over and over again.

Darcie Ann fluttered in and out of the front parlor like a nervous peahen until Virgie took her by the hand and said, "Christian and Laurel want to be alone, Mother."

And when they were alone, Laurel said, "Why didn't you call? Why didn't you tell me you were coming?"

"I took a late flight. I called your apartment as soon as I got to Atlanta. When you didn't answer I decided to come out here this morning."

"I'm surprised you remembered the way."

"I remember everything." His gaze met hers. "I've missed you," he said. "I've missed your laughter and your smiles, I've missed having breakfast with you, walking on the beach with you, swimming with you. I've missed you beside me when I go to sleep and when I awaken in the morning."

He took her hand. "*Grandmère* told me I was wrong to let you go. She told me..." he stopped, unable for a moment to go on "...she loved you."

"And I love her. I..." Laurel looked at him, her eyes gone wide with shock. "You said...you said she *loved* me."

Christian took her hand. "*Grandmère* died four days ago," he said.

Tears welled in Laurel's eyes. "Oh, Christian," she whispered. "You loved her so much. It must be so hard for you now." She stroked his cheek. "How did it happen? Tell me."

"She was working with her orchids. Etienne... Etienne was with her when she collapsed. He called to Solange and me." He took a steadying breath. "Thank God I was there. I'd never have forgiven myself if I hadn't been."

He waited a moment before he went on, then he reached into his inside breast pocket and drew out a small tissue-wrapped package. "She gave me this to give to you," he said.

Laurel bit down hard on her lower lip. She looked at Christian, then slowly unwrapped the tissue. The star sapphire, as blue as the Caribbean sky, winked up at her. "It's the ring Pierre gave her," she whispered.

"Yes, *ma chère.*"

She shook her head. "I can't. Solange should have it."

"Solange understands." He took Laurel's hand again. "Before *Grandmère* died she said that I was to give it to you. If you'll accept it, Laurel…" He looked at her, his heart in his eyes. "If you'll accept me."

For a moment she could not speak. She looked at the ring, then she raised her eyes to Christian's. "Oh, yes," she said. "With all my heart, yes."

They were married a week later on that sacred land that overlooked the Caribbean. It was a perfect island day; the sea was a clear and endless turquoise, the sky a cloudless blue.

Laurel wore a white satin wedding gown. She carried a bouquet of lavender orchids.

Dr. Verneuil acted as best man, Solange was Laurel's matron of honor. President Bazaine attended, as did most of the members of his cabinet and the parliament. Neither Laurel's sister nor her mother had come to St. Dominique for the wedding, but this morning Laurel and Christian had received a telegram wishing them happiness. Although there were still rough spots, Laurel hoped that in time they would come to accept Christian.

When the minister spoke of the meaning of love, they looked at each other and all that they were feeling was reflected in their eyes.

"Do you, Christian, take Laurel?"

"Do you, Laurel, take Christian?"

"I do," they said. "I do."

The minister spoke the words that united them as man and wife, and it seemed to Laurel that mingled with those words she heard the voices of all the people who had gone before, whispering upon the incoming tide.

A tide of change, she thought, for her and for him.

Christian lifted her veil. *"Je t'aime,"* he said.

"As I love you," she answered.

Then, while the guests waited, they went hand in hand to the sacred burial ground where Marie Dumond lay beside her husband, Pierre. Kneeling beside Christian, Laurel laid her bouquet of lavender orchids upon Marie's grave.

"Merci, Grandmère," she said.

Christian rested his hand palm down on the earth. Then he rose and drew Laurel up beside him. "I think she knows," he murmured.

"Yes," she said. And together they walked back to greet their guests.

*   *   *   *   *

Silhouette Books
is proud to present
our best authors,
their best books...
and the best in
your reading pleasure!

Throughout 1993, look for exciting books
by these top names in contemporary
romance:

CATHERINE COULTER—
Aftershocks in February

FERN MICHAELS—
Nightstar in March

DIANA PALMER—
Heather's Song in March

ELIZABETH LOWELL
Love Song for a Raven in April

SANDRA BROWN
(previously published under
the pseudonym Erin St. Claire)—
Led Astray in April

LINDA HOWARD—
All That Glitters in May

When it comes to passion,
we wrote the book.

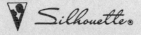

WHERE WERE YOU WHEN THE LIGHTS WENT OUT?

SILHOUETTE
SUMMER Sizzlers '93

This summer, Silhouette turns up the heat when a midsummer blackout leaves the entire Eastern seaboard in the dark. Who could ask for a more romantic atmosphere? And who can deliver it better than:

LINDA HOWARD
CAROLE BUCK
SUZANNE CAREY

Look for it this June at your favorite retail outlet.

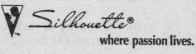

Silhouette®

where passion lives.

SS93